A NOVELIZATION BY
BRAD CARTER

BASED ON THE SCREENPLAY BY
ANDY SIDARIS

Encyclopocalypse Publications
www.encyclopocalypse.com

Foreword

If you're holding this book, odds are you know exactly what you're in for. Or maybe you just like your paperbacks hot, fast, and a little dangerous. Either way, welcome.

I grew up in the glow of late-night cable, where *Malibu Express* always felt like a secret handshake from another universe. Before streaming, before everyone knew what "cult classic" meant, Andy Sidaris movies were midnight transmissions from a world where the rules didn't matter. A world where a private investigator named Cody Abilene could outrun hitmen in a custom Chevy, flirt his way through a mansion full of suspects, and somehow solve the case...usually without putting down his Budweiser.

Malibu Express isn't just a time capsule of 1980s excess, it's the start of the Sidaris legacy: bullets, babes, wisecracks, and sun-drenched noir that never takes itself too seriously. Andy's genius was making it all look effortless. Fast cars, big hair, private islands, rocket launchers, and more silk robes than any one man should ever own...none of it accidental, and all of it a joy.

When Arlene Sidaris trusted us to adapt the catalog, it wasn't about nostalgia for its own sake. It was about keeping the party alive. A wild, sunburned celebration of everything that made these films feel forbidden and fun. Brad Carter starts us off on our literary Sidaris journey with *Malibu Express* and *Hard Ticket to Hawaii*, and he gets that. He's not just retelling the story; he's dialing in the sleaze, the smarts, and the strange sense of cool that makes Cody Abilene a fucking legend.

Why novelize Andy Sidaris films? Despite my own personal nostalgia and love of these films, we feel the world could use a little more bad behavior, a little more champagne, and a reminder that sometimes, the detective in the speedo is the only one who gets the job done. These books are for anyone who's ever rented a VHS just because the box looked a little too good to be true.

Thanks for picking this up and for keeping the Malibu Express rolling.

Sean Duregger
Managing Editor
Encyclopocalypse Publications

Chapter One

Cody Abilene stomped harder on the accelerator, gripping the wheel so tightly that his knuckles popped. The Chevy's heavily modified engine roared in response. The speedometer climbed past 120 mph and Cody forced himself to look away. Having grown up at auto racetracks, he knew all too well what would happen if he wiped out at that speed. Goodbye, Cody Abilene; hello, road pizza.

He thought of himself as a good driver. Under normal circumstances, he could handle just about any automobile, even at high speeds. After all, he'd won his fair share of drag races, of both the sanctioned and unsanctioned varieties. But these circumstances were anything but normal. For one thing, there was a topless woman riding shotgun, and she kept trying to climb onto his lap and press her considerable assets against his face. And for another thing, there was the small matter of the helicopter behind them. It was flying low in hot pursuit as Cody raced down the dusty two-lane desert road. He might have been able to deal with one of these complications, but both of them working in concert? That was just too much to juggle. Hell, even Cody's father—famed NASCAR driver Jimmy Dean

Abilene—couldn't have even approached peak performance under such circumstances.

The topless woman who wouldn't stay put in the passenger seat was June Khnockers, a rising star on the independent drag race circuit. It was Cody's considered opinion that June had a future as the first female NASCAR champion or a nudie magazine centerfold, possibly both. Her reflexes behind the wheel were just as impressive as her rack. And that was saying something. She was currently attempting to use that impressive rack to distract Cody from the task at hand. As far as distractions went, it wasn't so bad.

"Now, June, goddamn it, I can't do that right now," Cody snapped, swatting her hand away from his crotch.

"Oh, come on." June started to wriggle across the center console. She grabbed her breasts, pressing them together. "Don't you want to have a little fun?"

"Well, yeah, but..." Cody jerked his head to the side and narrowly avoided being blinded by one perfectly pink erect nipple. "Baby, this just ain't the time for it."

"It's always time to have fun!"

Cody had the car's engine cranked as high as he could manage. The needle of the tachymeter was crawling into the red. The engine temperature was doing the same. Something was wrong under the hood, and unfortunately, pulling over and letting the pit crew take a look wasn't an option.

Good Lord, can things get any more complicated? Cody wondered.

As if on cue, his thought was answered by a short burst of gunfire. The three idiots in the helicopter had opened fire. Cody figured it was coming, but he flinched all the same. At least the gunfire persuaded June to finally take their situation seriously. Her smile disappeared. She dropped back into the passenger seat, covering her breasts with her hands like she'd suddenly developed a sense of modesty.

"Oh my God, they're shooting at us!" she wailed.

"You noticed that, huh?" Despite everything, Cody had to laugh. "What do you think I've been trying to tell you for the last five miles, woman?"

"I'm sorry, it's just…" June tucked her goodies back into her jumpsuit and ran the zipper up.

Cody took a second to marvel at how quickly his life had gone off the damn rails. He thought back to where it all began. Was it really just a week ago?

Lord have mercy…

Chapter Two

Exactly one week before Cody was fending off a feisty half-naked woman while eluding a trio of helicopter-riding hired killers, he was enjoying a quiet Sunday. He spent the morning at the beach, watching the bathing beauties and the surfers. Once he'd done enough work on his suntan, he'd grabbed lunch from Tony Alvarez's hot dog truck, then headed to Vic's Gun Club to pop off a few rounds. It might have been a weekend, but that was no excuse for passing up a chance to work on one's marksmanship. And Cody was painfully aware of how much work he needed in that regard. As his daddy would have put it, Cody couldn't hit the broad side of barn.

He parked near the front door of the gun club and popped the trunk to get his gun. He stored the gun—a nickel-plated .44—in a beautiful gun case. It was zebra patterned Italian leather with a crushed velvet interior. He felt like a real stud carrying it into the club. Even the wealthiest members of the club admired it.

Vic's was a high class joint, frequented by doctors and lawyers and stock broker types. Cody maintained his membership as two birds/one stone deal: he could sharpen up his gun skills and make the kind of connections that any decent private detective needs. Not that Cody thought of himself as merely a decent private eye. No, he was top-shelf investigator for hire. It said so on his business cards, after all. Right there in black and white: *Cody Abilene, Top-Shelf Private Investigator.*

That day, there was no one on hand to admire his fancy gun case. Business at the club was slow on Sundays and Cody had the range all to himself, except for the club's resident instructor, John Strickland, an unsmiling gargoyle with Coke bottle specs and a meticulously maintained comb-over. If there was a high school in hell, Strickland would make a great vice principal.

"Good afternoon, Mr. Abilene," Strickland said. "How about taking lane number two. I assume you'd like the standard target."

Cody followed Strickland to the designated shooting lane. He set his fancy gun case on the ledge of the cubicle. The clasps made a solid *thunk-thunk* as he opened them. You couldn't beat those Italians for fine craftsmanship.

"I still say that .44 is too much gun for someone so…" Strickland looked up, like the word he was searching for might be on the ceiling. "Someone so accuracy challenged."

Cody ignored the implied insult and dumped a speed loader into the chamber of his Smith and Wesson beauty. He gave the chamber a spin and snapped it closed. Like the Italian leather case, the gun was a reflection of Cody's personality: cool, powerful, and just a little bit flashy. At least that's how he liked to think of it. He'd read somewhere that guns were just phallic symbols that men used to represent their manhood. That's what he got for leafing through old issues of *Cosmopolitan* while he waited for his turn at Fantastic Sam's.

Strickland sighed. "Okay, Dirty Harry, what will it be today, moving or stationary?"

"Moving."

Strickland brought out his heavy sigh for an encore. "You sure about that?"

"One hundred percent, my man." Cody put on his ear

protection, got into his stance, and prepared to take aim. Phallic symbol or not, the .44 was a heavy son of a bitch, so he used a two-handed grip.

"Here we go!" Strickland slapped a pair of protective earphones on his head and hit a switch on the wall, activating the moving target.

Two feet by two feet and made of cardboard, the target was printed with the outline of a human torso on its center. There was a bull's-eye over where the heart should be. The target hung from an overhead track by two lengths of monofilament line. Cody waited until it slid into his line of fire, then popped off a shot. The .44 jumped in his hands.

"Wide left, Mr. Abilene!" Strickland had to shout to make himself heard.

Cody tracked the target as it moved then fired again.

"Wide right!"

Cody narrowed his eyes and squeezed off two quick ones. He didn't need to hear Strickland hollering to know he'd missed the target altogether. The next two shots were just as bad. The last one went so high over the target that it shattered one of the overhead lights.

Strickland reeled in the target and presented it to Cody.

"Well, it's not my worst effort," Cody said, admiring his handiwork. The target had two bullet holes in it, although both of them were well outside the torso outline.

Strickland gave him a stern look over the top of the Coke bottle lenses. "Actually, I agree."

Cody tugged off his ear protection. They went into the fancy case, alongside the still-hot barrel of the .44.

"That's it?" Strickland asked. "Six shots and you're done?"

"I got places to go, partner."

The first place he had to go was the Willow Springs Raceway. It was a dinky little track out in the middle of the desert, but it had a certain charm. For weeks, June Khnockers had been using it for practice, and she'd been bugging him to come out there and watch her do speed tests in her new Oldsmobile stock car. She was practicing for an upcoming race in Baja and wanted Cody's opinion.

Yeah, that ain't all she wants, Cody thought as he wheeled his cherry red DeLorean into the raceway's back parking lot.

Even before he got out of the car, he could hear the steady roar of an engine cranked to maximum power. If he had to guess, June had it well over 120 mph, even on the curves. He had to admit it, the girl was good. Fearless with cat-like reflexes and a body that could stop traffic? God had been feeling generous the day he made June Khnockers.

Cody climbed the back stairs to the observation tower/announcer's booth and stepped onto the balcony. He walked through the empty booth and onto the balcony. Rodney Vargas was there, snapping photos of the action with one of her many cameras. This particular one had a telephoto lens so long it could probably double as an astronomy gadget. Her fingers danced around the apparatus, making adjustments to the focus as she took action shots worthy of the covers of all the trade magazines. Cody considered it one of the crimes of the century that *Car and Driver* hadn't offered Rodney a fat contract.

They went way back, Cody and Rodney. Once upon a time, she'd been on his father's pit crew, changing tires as fast as any man had ever managed. But she'd gotten tired of the life and traded her impact driver for a camera a few years back. Cody still caught up with her regularly, at the races or at one of the nearby bars. Despite their history, he'd never gotten a straight answer when he asked for the story behind her name. Cody figured it was sort of like the inverse of that old Johnny Cash tune. Rodney's daddy must have figured she'd have to get tough or die with a boy's name. Or hell, maybe it was the only name her parents could agree on. Either way, she was one hell of lady and one of the few who seemed immune to his amorous advances. Cody told himself that there were plenty of rumors about her batting from the other side of the plate, but deep down, he knew that his ego was the only reason he entertained such notions. And hell, if that was the way she wanted to swing, who was he to say anything about it?

Cody tiptoed across the metal balcony until he was alongside her. He draped his arm around her shoulders and leaned in to whisper a greeting in her ear.

If she was surprised, she didn't show it. She simply turned her camera toward him and took a shot of his face in extreme close up.

"You keep sneaking up like that, some lady is going to kick you in the goodies," she said.

Cody laughed. "You're one tough cookie, Rodney."

She stuck out her tongue and blew a raspberry. "Your biggest fan is just about to finish up for the day. I'm sure you'll be eager to rendezvous with her in the locker room."

"How do you know I'm not here just to see you?"

"Yeah, right. Even a Texas boy like you wouldn't survive this ride." Rodney laughed and went back to taking photos of June's car.

Cody hung around to watch the Olds hug the curves for a few more laps, then headed downstairs to the locker room. As such places went, this one wasn't so terrible. Sure, the aromas of BO and deodorant soap hung heavy in the air, locked in an eternal battle for supremacy, but the floor was clean enough and there was both a hot tub and a massage table on site. Cody removed his Stetson and his sunglasses, then hopped up on the massage table and lay down to wait for June to appear.

He didn't have to wait long. He'd just gotten comfortable when she entered the room. Even if she'd have been completely silent, he'd have known she was coming. June went through life with a cloud of expensive French perfume hanging over her.

Even after an afternoon spent sweating in her driver's jumpsuit, she still smelled good.

Cody sat up and watched he pause in front of her locker and start to undress. He whistled appreciatively.

"Well, is that all you got to say?" she asked, turning to face him. She unzipped her jumpsuit and pulled her arms free of the sleeves. Another quick move and her sports bra was gone, letting loose two double handfuls of fun.

For a moment, Cody was speechless as he took in the sights.

"Come on, what do you think?"

"I think they're dynamite."

She rolled her eyes. "I meant the driving."

"Same answer for the both the driving and the body," Cody said. "They're dynamite."

"You got a one track mind, cowboy." She kicked her way out of the jumpsuit's legs and crossed the space between the lockers and the massage table in a series of hip-rolling strides.

Cody smiled. "I reckon I'm just as God made me."

June leaned in for a kiss, then shoved him back down on the table. She had him out of his boots and his jeans in seconds flat.

"Now let's see if you can get me across that finish line," she purred.

As he drove away from the raceway, Cody figured the day had gone so well that it would be greedy to expect anything more. He drove the DeLorean back into town, steering with one hand and using the other to hold his mini tape recorder close to his face. He committed a short description of the day's activities to tape. The trade magazines said that all private detectives should own such a recorder and use it to keep track of daily activities. Of course, the article only meant that it should be done in the course of an investigation, and Cody hadn't been investigating anything beyond the June Khnockers' pleasure points, but he liked to get in the habit. If he wanted people to take him seriously as a detective, he needed to act the part. That's why he had the tape recorder, the fancy business cards, and a nickel plated phallic symbol loaded with hollow points.

Home was a 35-foot Sea Expedition yacht anchored at the Blue Sky Yacht Club's private marina. The yacht had one living room, one bedroom, a bathroom with a shower, and a bare-bones galley. None of them could be called roomy, but Cody liked to think of them as cozy accommodations. The yacht, which Cody had christened *Malibu Express*, was anchored with its stern against the dock. Cody had backed it up to that spot over a year ago and hadn't moved it since. Truth be told, he wasn't much of a sailor. He just liked the self-contained nature of yacht living. Plus, just about every sunset was postcard-worthy.

As he climbed out of the DeLorean, he noticed three figures standing on the dock, just a few feet away from the slip reserved for the *Malibu Express*. Cody recognized them right off. The tall one in the navy sport coat was Douglas Wilton, the president of the yacht club and superintendent of the marina. The two shorter figures, both clad in floral patterned Hawaiian shirts and white sailing caps, were the Martindales, George and his wife Claudia.

From what Cody could tell, the Martindales were haranguing good old Doug about some petty complaint. This came as no surprise to Cody. The Martindales were the marina's resident busybodies, who were always sore about something. At any given moment, they had a litany of grievances to air, many of which involved Cody and the *Malibu Express*.

As Cody walked down the dock towards his assigned slip, he learned that the subject of the Martindales' latest complaint was the large doorway that Cody had installed on the back of his yacht. Well, the doorway was actually built into a large square of Texas post oak which was anchored directly to the dock itself. Cody liked it. He thought it was a genius idea, a doorway that opened directly onto portion of the slip that abutted the stern of the yacht. The doorway was tasteful too, painted as it was to look like the caboose of an Old West train. Cody had paid a grad student at USC to do the work, and she'd earned every penny. Her skill with paints and varnish was outshone only by her skill in the bedroom.

Claudia Martindale was waving one pudgy hand at the door, calling it a "garish eyesore" when Cody drew up alongside Doug.

"Hey, Doug, how's it hanging?" Cody tipped his hat. He turned to Claudia and repeated the gesture. "Afternoon, ma'am."

Claudia, a hatchet faced woman with drooping jowls, put a hand to her chest and gasped. Her husband muttered and grumped. Cody favored him with a smile and was preparing to speak more pleasantries when Doug cleared his throat and jumped in.

"Mr. Abilene—er, Cody—this isn't the first complaint I've had about this monstrosity you've erected," Doug said. "As president of the yacht club, I must ask you to remove it."

"That's a shame," Cody sighed. "Most things I erect receive rave reviews. Just ask any of the ladies who've stepped through this doorway."

"And as members of the committee," George huffed, "we *demand* you do so immediately."

Cody shook his head. "Now, that's no way to talk. I should remind you folks that my daddy founded this yacht club over twenty-five years ago. On top of that, he built this doorway in loving memory of my mama, God rest her soul."

Doug didn't look impressed, and the Martindales seemed even less so. Claudia crossed her arms under her considerable bosoms, averted her gaze, and sniffed.

"Come on, Doug," Cody continued, "you know Daddy is at this very moment representing the yacht club in the TransPac. Got the club logo right there on the hood of his car, alongside the logo for Regina's Sandwich and Massage Shop. Where's the goodwill?"

"Some representation he's giving the club," George said, clapping a hand atop his goofy sailor cap to keep the wind from dragging it off his bald head. "He's lost four times in the last six days. Just what is he doing out there?"

"Well, he's got that all-girl crew, you know." Cody smiled. "Probably just keeps getting blown off course."

Doug's mouth twitched as he tried to stifle a smile. He turned to the Martindales and offered his best explanation. "You'll have to excuse Mr. Abilene. He's always been an eccentric young man. But he's telling the truth about this, well, art installation. Tacky as it may be, it is indeed a memorial to the late Mrs. Abilene. She was terrified of planes, cars, and boats. Trains, however, were something she loved. And to honor her memory, Cody hired a young up and coming artist to render this portrait of a locomotive."

Cody couldn't have said it better himself. Despite the Martindales' grumbling, he considered the matter closed. He tipped his hat to the trio, then stepped through the doorway and onto his boat.

He grabbed a beer from the fridge, and since he'd worked up quite a sweat during his encounter with June, he hit the showers. There truly were few pleasures in life more satisfying than a shower beer. It was the sort of thing that God had intended when he invented the pop top can.

Once he'd scrubbed himself clean and swallowed the last drop of Budweiser, he wrapped himself in a towel and headed for the galley to grab another beer... and found himself staring down the barrel of a gun.

"Goddamn, I sure hope that's a cigarette lighter," he said.

The gun-wielding assailant was a bikini-clad brunette. Standing close beside her was a similarly attired blonde. If they were burglars, they sure as hell weren't planning on hiding any stolen merchandise on their persons. Their bikinis didn't amount to much more than a few strings and some palm-sized scraps of fabric. Cody may not have cared their unannounced entry, but he approved of their fashion sense.

"Say your prayers, big guy," the brunette said and squeezed the trigger.

Cody closed his eyes against a spray of cold water. He snatched the squirt gun from her hand and tossed it over his shoulder.

"Cute toy," he said. "But I'm afraid I'm going to have to confiscate it."

The two women giggled as they moved to flank him, like they were preparing to pounce and wanted to cut off his escape route.

"I'm May," the brunette said. "And this here is my friend, Faye."

"We just arrived from Corpus Christi on my daddy's boat," Faye explained. "We're in the slip right next to you."

"Guess that makes us neighbors," May said. "Since we're gonna be here for a while, we figured we should get to know you."

Faye placed a hand on his shoulder. "It's the neighborly thing, after all."

Cody stepped across the room and lowered himself onto the loveseat, his new neighbors following close behind. They plopped down, one on either side of him.

"How the hell did you manage to get past my security system?" Cody asked. The system in question wasn't anything more than a lock on the door, but it was the best lock available at Ace Hardware. The salesman promised that it was made of American steel, which had to count for something.

"Never mind that." Faye scooted closer, pressing her thing against his. "We haven't got our water hooked up yet and wondered if we could use your shower."

May moved in, draping an arm over Cody's shoulders.

"Don't worry, we won't use too much water. We'll shower at the same time. You know, to practice conservation."

Cody smiled, glancing heavenward to offer silent thanks for his good fortune. It seemed that even on a day like this, there was always room for improvement.

"Well, ladies," he said, "never let it be said that an Abilene turned away in neighbor in need. Follow me."

Chapter Three

Contessa Luciana De Rossi pushed through the double doors of the California field office of the Federal Technology Crime unit at precisely 5:30 pm. She prided herself on her punctuality. Along with her keen fashion sense and even keener intellect, she considered her perfect timing to be her best quality. Well, her perfect timing and her perfect body, which she rigorously maintained through a strict diet and exercise regimen.

She slipped off her designer sunglasses and glanced at the front desk receptionist. "Contessa Luciana for Douglas Wilton."

The receptionist was a mousy young woman in an ill-fitting pantsuit. If time were not of the essence, Luciana might have tried to work the conversation around to fashion advice. Perhaps another day.

The receptionist nodded curtly. "Deputy Director Wilton is in the Strategic Ops office on the second floor. He's expecting you."

Luciana thanked the receptionist and headed for the elevators. Her high heels rang out like hammers on an anvil as she walked down the marble floors of the corridor. Every set of eyes she passed turned her way. This was such a regular occurrence that Luciana had long ago quit noticing the stares. She rode the elevator alone to the third floor. Upon arrival, she stepped out and headed for the Strategic Ops office.

Although it was a large room, it felt tiny, cluttered as it was with all manner of computer equipment. At this hour, most of the desks were empty. Even government security agents punched the clock at the end of the day. All that remained was a skeleton crew of the most dedicated operatives and engineers. They were so engrossed in their tasks that they didn't spare her a second glance. She tried not to take their disinterest amiss, even though she was wearing her newest, most flattering Versace ensemble.

She made her way through the maze of cubicles to the conference table at the back of the room. Doug Wilton, looking characteristically unfashionable in his navy blazer and khaki slacks, was waiting for her there. He didn't rise from his swivel chair or offer any pleasantries. As usual, he was all business when matters of national security were up for discussion.

"Have a seat," he said, gesturing to an empty chair on the opposite side of the table. "We have a real problem, Contessa."

"Let me guess," she said, dropping her clutch purse on the table and lowering herself into the chair. "This problem involves our Soviet friends."

"That's correct." Doug nodded. "The Russians are at least five years behind us in computer technology, but they're stealing our stuff right out from under us. We can't seem to get a handle on who's doing the dirty work. Could be government, could be organized crime. Over there, is there really much difference? Whoever it is, they've been working overtime to close the technology gap."

Luciana peeled off one black glove then the other. "Naturally. But how are they doing it?"

"First, they tried going through a bank in San Francisco, but the IRS was onto them before they could do much damage. Now, the bastards are setting up industrial fronts, buying stuff under the guise of supplying to our allies. Once the shipments make it overseas, Russian operatives embedded in the governments of these friendly nations clone the technology then send it along to Moscow. Our own agents in the Kremlin say that they've amassed quite a technological arsenal. It's just a matter of time before our own cutting edge gets back on us."

"Ah, yes, very intriguing," Luciana said, "but what has any of that got to do with me? I was having a nice vacation on the Riviera when I was recalled to this office."

Doug leaned forward, elbows on the table. "We've been investigating some of the players in computer research and development, trying to get a fix on who's dirty. I'll spare you the boring details, but the short version is that our investigation has led us to the doorstep of one of your old friends, Lady Lillian Chamberlain."

"Surely you're not suggesting that Lillian is involved in anything untoward..."

"All I'm suggesting," Doug said, "is that we need to get someone in there to figure out what the hell is going on. It can't be you, at least not directly. You're too high profile for one thing. And for another, you're too close to Lady Chamberlain and the rest of the household. They'd sniff you out in no time."

Luciana could see where this was heading, but she did as expected and stated the obvious. "I suppose you have someone in mind already or we wouldn't be having this conversation."

"That's right. I think I have the perfect candidate for this kind of work. In fact, I spoke to him just a few hours ago at the yacht club. I think you'll be impressed."

Luciana raised her meticulously plucked eyebrows. "And who might this impressive person be?"

"His name is Abilene," Doug said. "Cody Abilene."

Cody stood on the deck of the *Malibu Express*, munching on a hastily-assembled roast beef sandwich. Normally, at this time of night, he'd be enjoying his sunset view and maybe even some quiet fishing off the bow. But the evening's circumstances weren't normal, and it was far from quiet on board. May and Faye were giggling like schoolgirls as they played grab-ass in the shower. They also had the radio tuned to the local rock station and cranked up to the point that Cody was worried that his speakers might give out. It was a miracle that he even heard the insistent beeping of his brand new, digital read-out pager.

He tossed the scraps of his sandwich overboard to feed the fish and ducked back inside. The girls had finally shut off the water, but they hadn't dispensed with the giggling. On the deck, the radio had been a bit loud, but in the confines of the small living room, it was damn near deafening. Cody switched it off and grabbed his pager. He perched on the arm of the sofa and checked the pager's display. The message on the screen was from Douglas F. Wilton, and it was marked urgent.

His friendly neighbors stepped out of the bathroom and presented themselves for inspection, both of them naked as the day they were born.

"Cody, is it true you're a private investigator?" Faye asked, moving in so close that her nipple grazed his nose.

He had to summon every bit of his resolve to pull back from her. "Yes, darling, that's true."

"Then we want to hire you to investigate our privates," May said, pointing her fingers in the direction of what Cody often referred to as "the danger zone."

Once again, he called on his reserves of willpower and turned down the offer. "Look, ladies, I'd love to take your case, but it's just bad timing. I got some real work I gotta attend to, so you're going to have to scoot."

They retrieved their discarded bikinis from the floor and tugged them back on, complaining the whole time that he wasn't acting very neighborly anymore. He promised to take a rain check and cash it in at the first opportunity. They paused to shake their goodies at him one more time before departing.

"Goddamn, I should have my head examined, sending them away unsatisfied," he muttered as he watched them trot down the slip towards the painted caboose monument. "But duty calls."

The pager—a prototype on loan from one of Doug's government contacts—doubled as an answering machine. Cody had spent hours wondering how the little gadget actually worked before deciding his time was better spent contemplating the natural wonders of the world, specifically the seemingly endless parade of bikini-clad beauties cavorting on the sands of the nearby beaches. Technology may have been the destiny of mankind, but he just couldn't gin up enough enthusiasm to really delve into it. God bless the nerds, for they shall inherit the earth, as he liked to say.

He thumbed the button to play the message and was treated to a brief squall of static before the dulcet tones of the yacht club president/government agent took over.

"Cody, this is Doug. Sorry about that business earlier with the Marindales. Personally, I love the doorway, but you know how it is with them."

Cody laughed. Good old Doug, always trying to keep everyone happy.

"But enough about that," the message continued. "Let's get down to business. The agency has a very important job, and I think you're just the man for it. Your primary contact is Contessa Luciana De Rossi. She'll fill you in on the details. Now, I know what you're thinking, and the answer is yes, the Contessa is a very attractive lady. Try to be on your best behavior. I know that's asking a lot, but this is an important case. Here's the address of the house the Contessa uses when she's in town..."

Three hours later—just enough time to make himself presentable and stop at Larissa's House of Fashion for an ice-breaker gift—Cody parked the DeLorean in the driveway outside the Contessa's house. He opened the glove box and chose the best candidate from his collection of cologne bottles. "Nightshade Musk" it was called. The lady at the men's fragrance counter in the department store had assured him it was one of the year's hottest items. He gave himself a spritz, then collected the gift box from the passenger seat.

"All right, play it cool," he told his reflection in the rearview mirror, "Time to turn on that old Abilene charm."

He approached the front door with a spring in his step. It wasn't every day that a good old boy like him got the chance to mix with honest-to-God royalty. He just hoped Doug hadn't been stretching the truth about how attractive this Contessa was. Cody wasn't some cheap gigolo, after all; he had standards.

He'd barely finished knocking when the door swung open. It was all he could do not to gape at the woman standing there. Regal and statuesque in her high heels, with a head full of blonde curls and a body that scored 10s across the board, Contessa Luciana De Rossi was a vision to behold. Cody figured her picture could be found in Webster's Dictionary under the entry for "knockout."

He cleared his throat and said, "Good evening, Contessa. I believe you're expecting me. I'm-"

"Cody Abilene," she finished for him. "Please come inside."

He followed her into the house, getting an eyeful from the reverse angle. It was just as pleasant and the view from the front.

"I apologize for being so late, Contessa, but I wasn't familiar with the neighborhood," he confessed. "Truth is, I don't make it out this way very often. Not too many folks in my tax bracket do."

Her laugh was perfectly refined, just like the rest of her. "Oh, it's never too late to have a bit of fun. And please, call me Luciana."

"Well, Luciana," he said, handing over the gift box, "this is a little something I picked up for you. Had to guess at the size since all I had to go on was Doug's description, so I hope it fits. Something tells me that you'll bring some excitement to this simple frock."

"Why, thank you. I'll try it on right away. You can wait in the parlor while I change."

She led him into a sitting room that was roughly the size of a dance hall and invited him to have a seat on the massive leather sofa. Then she disappeared around a corner, leaving him alone in a room full of expensive furniture and decorated with fine art. He figured his annual income might cover one, maybe two of the paintings hanging on the walls. In a place like this, even the air felt expensive. He sat back and tried not to fidget. Although the dress he'd picked up—on Doug's tab, naturally— looked good on the mannequin, he wasn't quite sure how it would be received by a woman as sophisticated as Luciana. The outfit she already had on—a short black dress and a pair of ruby red high heels—had looked stunning enough. Maybe he should have gone with his first impulse and brought flowers instead.

All his doubts were obliterated at his first glimpse of Luciana as she re-entered the room in a series of slow, self-assured, hip-rolling strides. His whistle of admiration had passed his lips before he could rein it in. Apparently, the ladies at Larissa's House of Fashion hadn't steered him wrong. The silk dress hugged Luciana's body like it had been custom tailored for her. The ruby red fabric was a perfect match for her high heels.

"Douglas said you were a man of action," she said as she walked to the center of the room and did a slow turn. "But he didn't say you had such an elegant fashion sensibility."

Cody was proud of how fast he recovered and said, "It's not

so much the dress as it is the lady wearing it." He rose from the sofa and offered her his hand. "Shall we?"

It didn't take Cody long to figure out that Contessa Luciana subscribed to a "pleasure before business" philosophy. And that was just fine with him. The evening progressed from a candle lit dinner at the Burgundy Villa to cocktails and dancing at the Touch Club. Cody prided himself on his rhythm and grace, and was pleased to see that Luciana could match his energy on the dance floor. He was even more pleased to see that she could match his energy in a more intimate fashion when their night finished up in her bedroom.

As stunning as she'd looked in her new red dress, Cody preferred the way she looked without it. His eyes felt like they might bulge out of their sockets as they roamed from her full, pouty lips to her perfectly shaped breasts to her long legs. Another part of his anatomy bulged as his eyes continued their tour, moving from her feet—still wearing those glossy red high heels—to the junction of her thighs. When she let her hair down from the loose arrangement on top of her head and shook out those golden curls, Cody thought the sudden rush of blood to his nether regions might make him lose consciousness.

He did his best to work his way out of his suit and tie without taking his eyes off her.

"Here," she said, "let me help you."

Normally, Cody didn't need any assistance getting undressed, but he was happy for the help. With an extra set of hands doing the work, he was naked in seconds flat. Luciana damn near tackled him onto the king sized bed. Luciana may have been a refined, upper class lady who'd traveled the world, but Cody was certain he could give her an experience worth remembering. He gathered his strength and commenced mixing business with pleasure.

Cody figured out that not only should Mr. Webster have a photo of Luciana next to the entry for "knockout," but also one next to the entry for "insatiable." After an hour of going at it like a pair of drunk monkeys, he'd assumed they'd reached the end of the festivities. But judging from the way the Contessa was attempting to coax Cody Jr. back to life, she just thought they'd hit a lull in the action.

"Damn, woman," Cody moaned, detaching her hand from his pride and joy. "We keep this up, I'm liable to die from dehydration. I need some water."

She kissed him, then slid out of bed. "I'll bring you a Perrier."

"That's great, but really, tap water is fine. As long as it's wet, I don't care."

She paused in the doorway, still gloriously naked. "As long as it's wet, eh?"

Cody opened his mouth to respond, but she was gone before his brain could concoct the proper response. When she returned a couple minutes later, she was carrying a bottle of that fancy fizzy water and wearing floral-patterned kimono. Cody didn't know whether to feel relief or disappointment at her semi-clothed state.

She handed him the Perrier and climbed back into bed. Her kimono pulled loose, flashing Cody a glimpse of her bare breasts, but she drew it back together. The message was clear: the fooling around was over and it was time to get down to business.

"I'm not sure how much Douglas has told you about this operation," she said.

Cody took a slug of the water, wincing at the carbonation then sighing as it quenched his thirst. It was lemon flavored. Fancy stuff. He stifled a belch and told her that all Doug has said was that it involved the theft of computer technology, possibly by foreign agents.

Luciana nodded. "That's correct. One of our operatives tailed a suspected Soviet spy to a residence in Bel Air. It's unknown who this agent contacted or what his business in the residence was. Our operative was less than discreet, and the Soviet agent slipped his surveillance shortly thereafter. All further attempts to establish any sort of surveillance on the residence have met with complete failure."

Cody saw where this was going. "So either the Soviets are feeling the heat and you need to catch them before they change their operation up, or maybe it's just the rich folks keeping a lid on their own sordid secrets. And since the agency's high tech surveillance hasn't panned out, Doug decided to go the old fashioned route by putting a man on the inside. That about sum it up?"

"You're not just an excellent lover, you're also perceptive," Luciana said.

"Flattery will get you everywhere, Contessa. But tell me, why does the agency think sending a good old boy into high society is a good idea? Why not someone a little more, I don't know, refined? Like you, for instance."

"For one thing, these high society people, as you call them, will never see you coming. They'll underestimate you at every turn. Douglas tells me you graduated magna cum laude from the University of Texas. But these people won't know that. They'll see the hat and blue jeans, and they'll hear the accent, and they'll assume you're an ignorant hayseed. They just might let their guard down long enough for you to untangle this particularly stubborn knot."

"And here I thought my accent was disappearing after all this time in California," Cody said after another mouthful of fancy water.

"But the other reason I can't be involved in this investigation is that I know these people. The family matriarch is Lady Lillian

Chamberlain," Luciana explained. "As in the Chamberlain Plastics Corporation."

Cody whistled. "Big money."

"Lady Chamberlain and I go way back. She's nearly eighty years old, but still sharp. While I doubt she knows anything about Soviet espionage, she has the idea that something untoward is taking place amongst the cast of characters living on the family estate. She wants things cleaned up before people get a chance to read about it in the newspapers."

"And that's my cover, huh? Go in as a private investigator looking into the family, and maybe along the way I'll come across something involving theft of computer technology."

The Contessa smiled. "As I said, perceptive."

Cody shook his head. Doug Wilton never missed a trick. This was just the sort of out-of-left-field approach that might yield real results, so of course he had to do it through unofficial channels. It was a high stakes move that could get Cody hung out to dry, maybe even killed. But on the bright side, if he was working two angles, he could collect two paychecks.

He reached across Luciana to put his bottle of water on the nightstand. When he pulled his arm back, he loosened her kimono.

"Okay, if that concludes the business portion of the evening," he said, "how about we have an encore performance of the pleasure portion?"

Luciana was out of kimono and on top of him in two seconds flat.

Chapter Four

Cody stopped at the *Malibu Express* to take a shower and change clothes. It was time to get down to work, and it wouldn't do to show up for his first day on the job smelling like a French cathouse. Once he'd scrubbed and rinsed, he brushed his teeth, ran a comb through his hair, and put on his usual duds: ancient and faded Wrangler jeans, broken-in Justin boots, and an off-the-rack shirt purchased from western wear store in Lubbock. He paused on the way out the door to grab his Stetson and his sunglasses.

His new neighbors, May and Faye, were on the deck of their boat, listening to Pat Benatar on the radio and rubbing suntan lotion on one another. Despite his reserves being somewhat depleted after a night in the sack with the Contessa, he couldn't help but pause a few beats just to get an eyeful.

"Looking good, ladies!" he called as he turned away and continued on his way toward the dock.

"Where are you going?" Faye asked. "Don't you want to hang out with us for a while?"

"Yeah," May chimed in. "We can rub some lotion on you and talk about whatever pops up."

"No time," he said over his shoulder. "I gotta get to work."

He made it to the DeLorean before they could tempt him any further. The engine purred like the world's biggest cat as he put the car in gear and headed for the old state highway, which he preferred over the interstate. That familiar new case excitement was starting to take hold, reminding him of why he'd chosen this career over one in stock car racing. Both were exciting in their own ways, but detective work engaged his brain on a different level. To paraphrase the Contessa, he may have sounded like a hillbilly, but he was firing on all cylinders in the brains department, especially when it came to unraveling a mystery.

He grabbed the Bachman-Turner Overdrive cassette from the glove compartment and slotted it into the stereo. The bassline of "Not Fragile" had just started to thump out of the DeLorean's recently installed Blaupunkt 6x9s when an eggshell white Pontiac Sunbird and a beat-to-shit primer grey Ford pickup converged to cut him off at the junction of two stretches of dusty, sun-bleached blacktop. Cody stood on the brake and jerked the steering wheel to the right. The DeLorean's tires squealed, laying a streak of rubber on the asphalt.

"What the hell?" He opened the driver side door and stuck his head out to get a look at the collection of jackasses who'd nearly killed him.

He was more exasperated than shocked when he recognized the trio of idiots who disembarked their vehicles and made their way over to him. It was the Buffington clan, all three members.

There was the family patriarch, P.L. He was a short bowling ball of a man, perpetually sweating and red-faced, his bald head gleaming in the morning sun. Alongside him was his oversized wife, Doreen. She was packed into a floral print muumuu and her face was covered in makeup so thick that Cody figured she laid it on with a trowel. Bringing up the rear was their adult son Bobo. In the primate house at the local zoo, where Bobo's hygiene would have seemed appropriate, he might have been considered a deep thinker. Among normal folks, he was a common imbecile.

The Buffingtons looked to be pumped full of confidence as they swaggered up to the DeLorean's driver side window and launched into a tirade about challenging him to an impromptu race. At least that's what Cody thought they were shouting about. It was hard to know for sure, the way they were all hollering at once. Their excited voices rose in pitch and volume as they talked over one another. It was hard to tell if they were doing some sort of aerobic workout or just gesturing furiously.

Cody sucked in a deep breath, pursed his lips, and blew out a sharp whistle to shut them up before P.L. could work himself around to a heart attack.

"Damn, don't y'all ever take a break from acting the fool?" Cody asked when they paused to collect what little composure they could muster. "Now, P.L., since you're the most eloquent of the bunch, why don't you see if you can't explain just what the hell this is all about?"

"We got you now, boy!" P.L. exclaimed, bouncing from foot to foot. "We gone to tear you a new butthole! My boy 'bout to leave you chokin' on his dust!"

"Tell 'im, Daddy!" Bobo hollered.

Doreen chipped in her two cents by squealing and slapping her hands together like a trained seal.

"Race? In that thing?" Cody pointed at the Pontiac. "You can't be serious. I'll blow you off the road."

"Don't you worry 'bout that," P.L. huffed. "You just worry 'bout how you're gone to tell that daddy of yours how you lost a race to a Buffington."

"Are you telling me you're still sore about that?" Cody shook his head. "Good grief."

Thirty years ago, when both Cody and Bobo were still in diapers, Cody's father, Jimmy Dean Abilene, had beaten P.L. Buffington in a hundred lap qualifier in Charlotte. Jimmy Dean had gone on to a long, mostly successful NASCAR career, while

P.L. found himself relegated to the regional stock car circuit. Naturally, P.L. blamed his thwarted ambition on Jimmy Dean and had sworn revenge.

"What are you, chicken?" Bobo asked, hooking his thumbs under the straps of his overalls and flapping his elbows like wings.

"All right, then," Cody sighed. "Name the place."

"How 'bout right here and now?" P.L. suggested. "Go 'til the Fox Canyon cutoff. That's about what, three miles?"

"Fine by me," Cody sighed. "I was headed that way anyhow."

He lowered the DeLorean's door, twisted the volume knob on the stereo, and waited for Bobo to pull his Pontiac next the DeLorean. P.L. and Doreen waddled back to the truck. They piled inside and drove ahead to the finish line.

Cody glanced to his right and waited for Bobo to give him the nod, then he dropped the car into gear and hit the gas.

For the first mile, it was neck and neck. Cody held back, keeping it close for the moment. He figured he'd wait until the last half mile before blowing past Bobo. No sense embarrassing him in front of his parents, after all. Truth was, Cody kind of liked the old boy. Bobo was like a puppy that was too hyperactive and simple to be house-trained, but too entertaining to drop off at the pound.

But Cody's plan went awry when they came out of the curve just before the last half mile. The Pontiac let out a roar like a pissed-off grizzly bear. A thin stream of smoke puffed from the hood. And the car shot ahead, crossing the finish line a good two or three seconds before Cody's DeLorean.

Cody killed the volume on the stereo and cranked the window down. He drummed his fingers on the steering wheel and let the Buffingtons gloat about their victory. After he'd given them a suitable amount of time to get it out of their systems, he raised his hands in defeat.

"Well, y'all just remember the Alamo, I guess," he said. "I'll get you next time. But right now, I got places to be."

They were still dancing like fools when Cody drove off. He glanced into the rearview mirror and chuckled at the spectacle of the three idiots carrying on like pack of escaped lunatics. The little Pontiac was still venting smoke or steam, maybe both. No doubt about it, something was wrong. Either Bobo had done some heavy duty modification to that Sunbird or there was something wrong under the hood of the DeLorean. Probably the former. From the way the Sunbird's engine had damn near exploded, Cody suspected Bobo had been fooling around with nitrous oxide. Still, it was better safe than sorry, so Cody decided to make a quick detour to Mitch Harris' garage.

Mitch was the best kept secret in the world of engine repair. He was the only one Cody trusted with the DeLorean. His garage was a greasy, cluttered mess, just like its owner, but it was like the Mayo Clinic for automobiles.

"Don't you worry baby, we'll get this figured out." Cody gently patted the DeLorean's dashboard as he pulled into the lot. He parked outside the garage and went off in search of the proprietor.

Mitch was deep into a complete rebuild of a Mustang's ailing engine, but he said he'd get to the DeLorean just as soon as he was done.

"Thanks a bunch, Mitch," Cody said, tossing him the keys. "She just got beat by a little Pontiac four-banger and I need to know if something's ailing her."

Mitch tucked the keys into the pocket of his coveralls. "Sure thing, Cody. Soon as I get this Mustang squared away. Case you were wondering, I'm almost done with your dad's Olds. Made a few special modifications. Nothing street legal, if you want to be picky about it, but I guarantee you no four-banger will even come close to beating that Olds once I'm through with her. Should only take me another day or two."

"Fine by me." Cody glanced around the parking lot. "You got a loaner I can drive meantime?"

"Got that black beauty." Mitch gestured with a grimy hand at a Ford Pinto with a dented left quarter panel. "Keys are already in it."

"I reckon beggars can't be choosers." Cody shook his head.

"Come on, now, she's not as bad as she looks," Mitch laughed. "Well, okay, maybe this is one of those times where you actually can judge a book by its cover. But hell, the price is right."

As much as it pained Cody to admit it to himself, he felt like a damn fool parking that Pinto outside the Chamberlain estate. At least the guard at the neighborhood's front gate had let him through without any hassle. Apparently, Cody was on the guest list.

There were other cars parked in front of the massive house. A black Bentley, a candy apple red Alfa Romeo Spider, a snow white Caddy, and a shit brown Jaguar. Ugly as that Jag was, it would still beat the Pinto by a country mile in a beauty contest.

Sure miss my DeLorean, Cody thought as he trotted up the front steps and rang the doorbell. Judging by his black suit and severe expression, the fella who answered the door was either some sort of butler or an undertaker. The look he gave Cody was just one notch shy of outright hostility.

"Nice car," the butler remarked, staring over Cody's shoulder at the Pinto.

"Yeah, well, I figure with my good looks and charming personality, no one much cares what I'm driving, right?" Cody handed the man his Stetson. "Name's Cody Abilene. Lady Lillian is expecting me."

"You're late." The butler hung the Stetson on the nearby

coatrack the door and stepped aside just enough to let Cody in. "She's out by the pool. Follow me."

Cody did as he was asked, although he didn't care much for the man's tone. In general, Cody liked to give people the benefit of the doubt. Maybe the guy had a sour stomach. Then again, maybe he just had a sour disposition. Not everyone could be a beacon of joy like Cody.

Strolling through the house was like taking a walk through a museum. Every piece of furniture looked like it had been arranged for a photo shoot. The floors were so polished that they squeaked beneath Cody's feet, which was saying something since he was wearing boots.

The butler opened the back door and led him across a wide patio to where Lady Lillian was seated poolside. Her right leg was encased in a plaster cast, a souvenir from her recent tumble during her annual ski trip to the Swiss Alps, and she was seated in a wheelchair.

"Cody Abilene," she said, giving him a quick appraisal. "How nice to make your acquaintance."

He extended his hand and she gave it a light squeeze. Cody didn't quite know how this sort of handshake was supposed to go. Mixing with such refined company wasn't an everyday activity in his world.

Lady Lillian finally let go and turned to look up at her stone-faced butler. "Shane, fetch Mr. Abilene's bags from his car and take them to the guest room with the Picasso on the wall."

The butler, Shane apparently, nodded curtly then turned on his heels and made himself scarce.

"That guy's a real charmer," Cody said.

Lady Lillian smiled and motioned for him to take a seat in the chair on her right. "It takes Shane a while to warm up to new faces. I suppose I should tell you that he's not overjoyed to have you in the house. He thinks I'm crazy for suspecting that anything untoward is taking place under my roof."

Cody nodded, filing that information away. In his experience, only people with something to hide were made uncomfortable by the presence of a private investigator. Most people just wanted to know if his life was anything like *Magnum P.I.*

"And if he can't be polite, well, I'll just remind him of who signs the paychecks around here," Lady Lillian said.

Cody laughed. He'd only just met her, but he could already tell he was going to get along with Lady Lillian just fine. Luciana had said that she was a tough old bird and sharp as a tack. Their families, the Chamberalains and the De Rossis, had been friends for two generations. The Chamberlain fortune was made in plastics, and the De Rossi family got rich importing them to Europe.

"You came highly recommended, Mr. Abilene," Lady Lillian said, gazing at the breeze-rippled surface of the swimming pool. "Contessa Luciana De Rossi speaks very highly of you, and I have complete faith in her judgment."

At least a half dozen witty remarks about Luciana sprang to Cody's mind, but he resisted the urge to speak a single one. He settled for saying that he hoped he could live up to her expectations. He also told her that he wasn't entirely sure what he was investigating.

"Well, that's just the thing," she said. "I can't put my finger on it, but I just know there's something going on behind my back. With so many people living under one roof, that's probably inevitable, I suppose. There's my nephew Stewart and his wife Anita, plus my niece Liza. They've all lived here since their parents died in that plane crash back in 1975. Of course, there's also Shane, who you've already met, as well as my maid, Marian. She and Shane came as a package deal. The kitchen staff and gardeners don't live in the house, but you might see them around."

"Quite a crowd," Cody agreed.

"And quite a cast of characters. Just wait until you meet Marian. She's positively out to lunch." Lady Lillian shook her head, then continued, "To be perfectly honest, I'm not sure I trust any of them. That's a horrid thing to say about people who've lived with you for ten years, and most of them blood relations, but it's the truth. Here's another truth, Mr. Abilene: I'm not getting any younger, and if I'm going to include these people in my will, I want to know that they can be trusted to manage the estate properly. My grandfather didn't build the family fortune just to have it squandered."

Cody nodded. "Fair enough. If there's something shady going on, I'll sniff it out. And please, call me Cody."

He had one more thought that he didn't vocalize: if those shady dealings Lady Lillian was so worried about happened to involve the sale of computer technology to Soviet agents, being left out of the Lady's will would be the least of the family's concerns.

Anita Chamberlain was supposed to be playing tennis at the country club her Aunt Lillian owned, but she didn't really care for tennis. When it came to getting an aerobic workout, she much preferred her current activity: making vigorous, sweaty love to the butler/chauffeur, Shane. They were in one of the estate's three guesthouses, going at it on top of the pool table. Anita was bent over, her cheek pressed against the felt surface as Shane gave it to her from behind.

"That's it, baby," she moaned. "Keep going, I'm almost there…"

Shane grunted wordlessly, pushing harder without breaking his rhythm.

What he lacked in personality, Shane more than made up for in stamina and creativity. It was hard to believe someone so otherwise dull could possess the imagination necessary for some of the positions he'd introduced her to. If only he wasn't such a grunting Neanderthal…

But that was the thing, wasn't it? If she wanted anything

approaching sexual satisfaction, she had to take what she could get. Stewart certainly wasn't up to the task. He was, as Shane so delicately put it, light in the loafers. Anita had known about it for years, ever since she caught him and one of the country club's golf pros in bed together. Once she'd gotten over her initial outrage, Anita had adopted a more pragmatic view. If Stewart wanted to play with the boys, she was happy to be his alibi. And if she wanted to get her rocks off outside the bonds of matrimony, he didn't have a say in the matter. Of course, it didn't hurt that Stewart's aunt was filthy rich and Stewart stood to inherit at least a portion of the Chamberlain estate.

The mental pleasure of knowing that she'd one day be filthy rich combined with the physical pleasure of Shane's tireless thrusting was a potent cocktail. Anita screamed and shook as she climaxed. Shane let himself go. To Anita's ears, his moans sounded as much like relief as pleasure. And when he pulled out and she slid off the table, the look on his face didn't show a hint of satisfaction. That was fine with Anita. As long as she was taken care of, she didn't give a damn about him.

She went to the bathroom to wipe herself down and check her hair. There was a bottle of perfume on the sink, which she kept there for these little trysts. She spritzed herself, hoping that Chanel No. 5 was strong enough to mask the sex smell.

When she stepped out of the bathroom, Shane was already dressed. The expression on his face was as impassive as ever.

"You better clean up better than that before dinner," he said. "Lady Lillian says she wants the entire family to have dinner in the main dining room. Guess she wants to impress that private dick she invited to stay here."

Anita raised her eyebrows. "Oh yeah?"

"Don't get too excited," Shane sniffed. "You're probably not his type."

"How would you know anyway?" She brushed past him, heading for the door.

Chapter Five

Cody wondered if all the family dinners at the Chamberlain estate were this awkward or if the family was putting in extra effort on his account. If that was the case, they sure as hell succeeded. The tension in the air was as thick as the potato soup served as the first course. The conversation was light, yet everyone's delivery was terse, the pauses pregnant. It didn't take long for Cody to have them pegged. The nephew, Stewart, was nice enough, but he was queer as a three-dollar bill. Cody would have bet the DeLorean's pink slip that Stewart preferred the company of men. And that was a shame, because his wife, Anita, seemed like a woman who liked a good time. Before that thick-as-wet-concrete potato soup even hit the table, she was on her second glass of wine and her second joke, this one involving a priest, a rabbi, and an Italian stable boy. Lady Lillian was clearly horrified at the punchline, shaking her head in disapproval while Cody tried not to laugh.

Lady Lillian's younger niece, Liza, didn't arrive until Shane had cleared the soup bowls to make room for the main course. The maid, Marian, walked a slow circuit of the table, refilling water glasses. Cody tried not to stare. When Lady Lillian had said Marian was a character, she'd made the understatement of the year. Marian had an outrageous mane of wavy blonde locks that hung to her waist. She spoke in a lilting, sing-song voice that made everything sound like the question from the mouth of a bewildered child. If Cody had to guess, he'd say she was on one or more illicit substances.

The food on the plate looked pretty good—it was steak with some sort of wine sauce—but Liza looked even better. If Cody had to use one word to sum her up, it would be "perky." She had a perky nose, perky tits, and a perky personality to match. She practically skipped across the dining room, babbling some convoluted excuse for her tardiness, and dropped into the vacant chair across the table from Cody.

"So nice of you to join us," Lady Lillian said.

"Yeah, yeah, yeah, sorry I'm late," Liza replied. "You know how it is."

The look Lady Lillian gave her niece could have melted ice at a hundred yards. "Liza, this is Cody Abilene, our houseguest."

Liza dropped swept her napkin off the table and dropped it in her lap. She grabbed her fork with her left hand and poked it into her mashed potatoes. "Yeah, I noticed your car. It's quite a showpiece. Takes real confidence to drive something like that."

"Thanks." Cody wasn't taking that bait. "You know, I really like to drive."

Anita, seated at Cody's left, giggled. "I just bet you do. I bet you're a real hard driver."

Cody's brain went into overdrive to formulate the proper response. His mental engine locked up when he felt Anita's hand groping his thigh beneath the table.

Liza bailed him out, asking, "Cody, do you like to cook?"

He cleared his throat. "To be honest, I'm not much of a cook."

She lobbed another question at him. "Well, what do you make for dinner?"

"Reservations," he replied.

The line earned him laughs all around. Even Stewart, whose expression constantly suggested he'd gotten a mouthful of something sour, let out a giggle.

Cody gave them his best good old boy smile, but all he could think about was how goddamn strange rich folks could be.

Cody left the estate as soon as Marian cleared away the dessert dishes. He had a standing date with his cop friend, Sergeant Beverly McAfee. Every Tuesday and Thursday, they met at Gold's Gym for a nighttime workout. Most nights, they went dancing afterwards. More often than not, one thing led to another, and they got in a second workout that was just as vigorous and sweaty as the first, only far more pleasant. This particular Tuesday, Bev was pulling a double shift, which meant she had to go back to the precinct after they finished.

"Don't they ever give you the night off?" he asked Bev as he spotted her while she did an incline press.

"No rest for the weary, Cody." Bev pushed the bar up, held it for a moment, then lowered it slowly.

A couple of showoffs pumping free weights just a few feet away glared at Cody with undisguised contempt. They stage whispered to one another as they knocked out hammer curls. The topic of this stage whispering was Cody, specifically how such a "pencil necked little boy" could catch the eye of a "hot piece of ass" like Bev.

"Hey, fellas," Cody said, glancing their way as Bev tried for another rep. "No offense taken, just in case you were wondering."

The two muscleheads stared at him, clearly shocked that anyone would dare speak to them in such a manner. One of them was a black dude who was built like the damn Incredible Hulk. His muscles had muscles. His partner looked like a bargain store version of Sylvester Stallone and a laugh like the slowest kid in a remedial class.

Cody waved at them. He considered blowing a kiss, but figured he'd better not push his luck.

"So how's this case you're working?" Bev asked. She dropped the bar back on the rack and sat up. "Anything exciting?"

Cody shrugged. "Rich people and their bullshit. You know how it goes."

"I just bet they love having that Pinto parked outside their mansion," Bev laughed.

"Hey, it's a loaner."

Shane was officially off the clock, but he still had plenty work to do. After dinner was over and that annoying private detective had excused himself, Shane stopped at his room in the servants' quarters just long enough to shuck his butler uniform and throw on a pair of shorts and a t-shirt. Since Marian lived in the main house and the other staff left the estate when they were off duty, Shane was the sole occupant of the servants' quarters. They didn't amount to much more than a bungalow, but they were private, and that's what mattered most to Shane.

He grabbed one of his cameras—a slick Vivitar with an auto focus and timer function—then headed for the main house. He didn't bother sneaking around. At this hour, no one would spot him creeping into Liza's room.

He smiled to himself when he heard the sound of a running shower coming from Liza's bathroom. This was going to be easier than he thought.

Liza was off in her own world, singing some stupid pop song while she soaped herself up. The details of her naked body were blurry through the semi-transparent shower curtain and the thick fog of steam, but the little bit Shane saw was enough to get his motor going. The counter was strewn with what appeared to be an entire cosmetics store's inventory of makeup, lotions, and hair products. Shane shook his head in dismay as he cleared a spot for the camera. These rich broads were all the same. Vain and stuck-up and bitchy. But deep down, they were just like the girls he picked up while cruising Sunset. They wanted it just as badly. Hell, maybe they wanted it even more.

He checked the camera to make sure it was set up to snap a photo every ten seconds, then pulled the shower curtain back.

"You know, back when I was in the joint, I swore I'd never take another group shower," he said, stepping into the hot spray of water. "But there was no one like you in Pelican Bay."

"Shane! What are you doing?" Liza squealed, pressing herself into the corner.

"What's it look like, baby?" He grabbed her hand and guided it to his equipment. "Better yet, what's it feel like?"

She shook her head and protested, but her hand lingered long enough to let Shane know her resistance was just a show. Like he told himself just a moment ago, these rich broads wanted it just as much as any woman. It only took a few more seconds for Liza to hit her knees and get to work. Shane glanced over at the camera and smiled as the shutter clicked. What a nice little photograph that was going to be. He grabbed her shoulder and brought her to her feet. She moaned as he turned her around so he could give it to her from behind. The way she moaned, Shane figured she liked it this way just as much as her sister-in-law. Maybe they had more in common than they let on.

When they finished up a few minutes later—not Shane's best performance, but far from his worst—he and Liza washed themselves off. The camera clicked a couple more times before it reached the end of the film roll. A few more shots to complete the collection. There was a time when Shane might have felt a twinge of guilt. Liza wasn't so bad as far as spoiled rich girls went. She was only twenty-one, so she hadn't gotten to that stage where she was bored and casually popping pills and drinking herself to death the way so many of them ended up. But the time when Shane felt guilt was long gone. Now he looked at Liza and just saw a stepping-stone. Yeah, okay, a stepping stone with a nice set of tits and an ass like two bags of firmly packed sugar, but a stepping stone all the same. These days, dollar signs got him harder than tits and ass.

He climbed out of the shower and wrapped a towel around himself.

"Hey," Liza asked, confused. "Where are you going?"

Shane held up the camera so she could get a good look at it. "Thanks a lot. I enjoyed it."

She squealed indignantly and started calling him every name in the book. Shane didn't mind. He knew he was a son of a bitch. He just didn't care.

Across the hall, Stewart was trying to sleep. He was simply exhausted after another day trapped in this garish house with his tiresome family, but he still couldn't fall asleep. His brain wouldn't turn off. His imagination—overactive was an understatement—kept conjuring up images that goosed his heart rate. That private detective, for instance. With that mustache and the cowboy boots, he gave Stewart a thousand naughty thoughts. Cody Abilene was clearly straight as an arrow, but a man could still dream.

Anita didn't seem to have any trouble sleeping. Just a few inches away, she was lying on her back, snoring with her mouth open. The blankets had pulled down just enough to expose her breasts. The woman insisted on sleeping in the nude, no matter how much Stewart told her that it bothered him. He rolled his eyes. Anita was such a slob. She may have possessed a swimsuit model body, but she was still just a colossal bore with bad fashion sense. Apart from covering for his proclivities, she was basically useless. He shuddered as he ~~tugged~~ covered her back up with the blanket.

He was just weighing the pros and cons of popping a Valium when he heard a faint ruckus across the hall. It sounded like shouts coming from Liza's room.

What is that little slut up to now, I wonder? Stewart thought.

He got out of bed, careful not to wake his slob of a wife, and tiptoed to the bedroom door. He opened it slowly, just a crack, mindful of the occasionally squeaky top hinge, and peered into the dimly lighted hallway. Liza's door swung open, and out walked that hunky dolt Shane.

Stewart wrinkled his nose. He had history with the butler and didn't care for him one bit. Shane strutted around like he was cock of the walk, when he wasn't anything more than hired help. Plus, that whole macho ex-con thing didn't fool Stewart one bit. He happened to know that Shane didn't mind swinging the other way when it suited him. Still, he had to admit, the butler was quite a specimen, if you went in for that rough-around-the-edges-handyman look.

Ugh, Stewart shuddered. Once bitten, twice shy.

Wrapped in a towel and hair still dripping, Shane looked like he was fresh from the shower. He paused outside Liza's door and laughed like he'd just thought of some private joke.

Well, now there's an interesting development... Shane and Liza, huh?

Stewart heard the faint rustle of sheets behind him and quickly shut the door. He turned around and saw his wife sitting up in bed. She stretched languidly, raising her arms over her head. The movement put her breasts on full display once again. Stewart couldn't help but think she was doing it just to torment him. He wondered how she could stand it. Didn't carrying those things around give her back trouble?

"What are you doing over there?" she asked.

"Oh, nothing," Stewart answered. "Just thought I heard a noise."

Chapter Six

Cody finished swimming laps then spent a few minutes floating on his back, looking at clouds like pulled-apart cotton balls as they drifted across the blue sky. The sun's rays poked through, making him wish he hadn't left his shades on the dresser in his room. It had been a pleasant morning and it was melting into a pleasant afternoon. He was beginning to feel guilty for collecting a paycheck when all he'd done so far was eat expensive food and swim.

"Hey, there," a voice called, pulling him out of his aimless daydreaming. "Feel like joining me for lunch?"

Cody shaded his eyes and looked across the pool. Liza was seated at the big picnic table, looking like she'd just come from the tennis court in her white shorts and sleeveless shirt. Her sneakers looked brand new and the bracelets on her wrist certainly hadn't come from the drugstore jewelry counter. She had the *New York Times* in her lap. It was folded back to the crossword puzzle and she was tapping at with the pen in her left hand.

Cody swam to the edge of the pool and levered himself out of the water. He scooped his towel off the nearby chaise lounge and wrapped it around his waist.

"Who could turn down a poolside lunch with a pretty lady?" he said, lowering himself into the chair across from Liza. "That Sunday puzzle can be a real bear. Takes me all day sometimes."

"Yeah, well…" She tossed the newspaper and the pen on the table. "You're not just a pretty face. Is that what you're trying to say?"

Cody shrugged. "Take it however you like."

Marian appeared like she'd been summoned by some secret signal.

"We have fresh escargot or chicken salad on croissants available," Marian said in her strange lilting delivery.

Liza asked for the escargot, which made Cody shudder.

"Guess I'll have the chicken salad," he told Marian. "I don't eat anything that leaves a trail."

Marian gave him a strange look then departed.

"She's a strange one, isn't she?" he asked.

"You can say that again. It's like she's from another planet," Liza laughed. "That hair and that voice…"

A short interval of awkward silence passed between them. Cody could have sworn that Liza was working herself up to telling him something but kept talking herself out of it. Something about the way she kept looking at him then glancing away, her mouth open ever so slightly. He had to guess, he'd say she was one of Lady Chamberlain's prime suspects for bad behavior. At the very least, she had more than her share of secrets. Cody could tell that much just looking at her. She certainly was pretty, though.

Finally, Marian reappeared and plunked their lunch plates and two sets of silverware rolled into white napkins on the table. She swished away, humming to herself. Liza moved her bundle of silverware from the right side of her plate to the left.

"I swear, that woman has the memory of a goldfish," Liza said. "She's been here for five years and still can't remember that I'm a lefty."

Cody shrugged. "I hear good help is hard to find."

"I wouldn't know. My aunt does the hiring and firing around here."

"How's your day been so far?" Cody asked, wincing as Liza forked a snail into her mouth.

"You don't have to be nice to me, you know," she said. "It's not part of the job."

"Oh, I insist on it. Us Texas boys are known for it."

"Well, that's bullshit, but I guess I don't mind." She sighed, shaking her head. "Of all days to be stuck here. My Mercedes is in the shop and I really need to get to Palm Springs."

Cody finished chewing his bite of sandwich, then said, "What about Shane? Isn't chauffeuring part of his gig here at the estate?"

Liza's face darkened with disgust at the mention of the butler's name.

"Forget that son of a bitch," she said. "I don't want to be anywhere near him. Besides, he's too busy slipping it to my sister-in-law. I believe you Texans call it 'laying pipe'? Shane and Anita are like a couple of horny teenagers, always sneaking off to the beach house to get it on. Sometimes, I guess they can't contain themselves, and they do it in Shane's room. I've seen Anita doing the walk of shame from the servants' quarters to the main house plenty of times."

"Really?"

"Oh yeah." Liza nodded. "A couple weeks ago, I thought I might go for a walk on the beach. I was going to stop by the beach house to grab some suntan lotion and nearly walked in on them. But I could hear them as soon as I opened the door. Sounded like the set of a porno movie. *Yeah, baby, give it to me* and *Oh, Shane, it feels so good…* gross. I don't know why they bother. It's not like it's a secret around here. Well, I don't think my aunt knows, but otherwise…"

"How's Stewart feel about that?" Cody asked.

"Oh, come on. It's not exactly a secret that my brother is as fruity as the produce department. You're not much of a detective if you didn't pick up on that." She paused just long enough to chew up another snail, then asked, "You got any brothers or sisters?"

"Got a cousin named Rowdy. Two years younger than me," Cody answered. "My uncle died when Rowdy was just a kid, so my daddy raised him. Guess he might as well be my brother."

"Then you know what a pain in the ass they can be. Some days, you can't decide whether you love them or want to spike their Perrier with strychnine."

Cody smiled. He liked this girl. "Well, if you don't mind being seen in a Ford Pinto, I can give you a ride to Palm Springs."

"Would you, really? I don't want to be a bother."

"It's no bother. My schedule is wide open today. You don't mind me asking, what's so important in Palm Springs?"

"No big deal," Liza said. "I just wanted to see a friend who lives there."

If Shane had taken it easy on Liza the night before, it was just because he was saving his strength for Anita. Sex with her could be more like an athletic event than lovemaking. It was the reason he kept a couple bottles of Gatorade in the beach house refrigerator. If the mood caught Anita just right, she could send you in the hospital for dehydration.

But Shane didn't mind. He liked a woman who could match his energy. Plus, she was about as well put together as a woman could be. Certainly better looking than any of his past girlfriends. And that's why it was such a bummer that their encounters had become part of his blackmail scheme. Once that cat was out of the bag, it would be all she wrote on their purely carnal relationship. No way was he going to continue an affair with a scorned woman. He wouldn't even be able to enjoy a blowjob without being afraid she'd bite it off.

They were in their usual spot—the beach house—going at it like their lives depended on it. And they'd been at it for a good half hour already, ever since Anita had wrapped up her late morning tennis match with Liza. At this hour, Shane was supposed to be taking inventory in the wine cellar. But he felt like he was in the clear, at least as far as Lady Lillian was concerned. Not like the old bag could roll that wheelchair down the stone staircase that led to the cellar.

"Oh, baby," Anita moaned. "I want you to give it to me hard..."

Shane almost whimpered. He didn't know that he could dish it out much harder without doing serious damage to his lower back. But he played along, talking dirty while he glanced around the room to make sure his cameras were functioning. He may have trusted his shower with Liza to his handheld Nikon, but that Liza was just a bonus. The real score was Anita, and that meant using his full setup to capture her from all angles. There were two cameras taking still photos: one peeking out through a hole in the headboard and another in the closet. The real jewel was the video camera hidden behind the dresser across the room. One touch of the remote control, and out it popped, ready to capture their sex marathon in full color, direct to VHS tape.

"Come on, let's switch up," Shane gasped, pulling out.

"Yeah, I want to be on top." Liza practically wrestled him onto his back. She swung her leg over his pelvis and climbed on.

Shane let out a satisfied sigh. Not only would this give him a bit of a break, it would also provide a new camera angle. A two birds, one stone kind of thing. He loved it when things were easy.

Liza had never ridden in a car as broken down and pathetic as Cody's Pinto. But all things considered, it wasn't so bad. The Pinto must have been missing whatever part kept a car from bouncing like a carnival ride at the slightest bump in the road, but even that wasn't so bad. It was actually sort of fun and made the normally boring drive to Palm Springs an adventure. Especially because Cody didn't take the interstate, choosing to navigate a maze of back roads that Liza never knew existed.

Cody was a good driver. He'd told her he grew up on the race car circuit and it certainly showed. Even though he had the Pinto doing ninety—probably the car's top speed—he drove one-handed with apparent ease. The air conditioner was broken, so he also drove with the windows halfway down. Some dust and road grit blew in, but even that was okay. She leaned her seat back and threw one foot up on the dashboard.

"You must have a road atlas in your head," she said. "I never even knew there were roads like this around here."

Cody favored her with his cowboy grin. "Well, thanks, I guess. I suppose growing up with a stock car driver for a father gave me a keen sense of direction."

"I bet that was fun. My father worked for an investment firm. I saw him for a few hours every week, whenever he could tear himself away from the office. He wasn't much fun."

"Some people might say that fun ain't everything. Maybe they're right, I don't know." Cody shrugged. "So, who's this friend we're driving all this way to see?"

Liza hesitated for a moment. She didn't know if she should be nervous discussing this sort of thing with Cody or not. He was a detective, after all. But what the hell, she figured. He was just doing some grunt work for Aunt Lillian, probably making sure Shane, Marian, and the rest of the help weren't stealing silverware or something. The old lady was paranoid about that kind of thing.

"His name's Jonathan Harper." Liza dug a pack of French cigarettes out of her purse and used the Pinto's lighter to get it going. "Jonathan's in computers. He sells them worldwide. And he's got this new company he's starting. They're going to develop new computer systems. I don't really understand all of it, but I do understand that stuff is the wave of the future."

Cody gave her a look. "You know, lots of folks in that line have been caught doing shady deals with communist countries. I assume your friend's legitimate."

She exhaled a plume of smoke in his direction. "Jonathan's reputation is fine by me. And besides, I asked you to drive, not give me your opinion on who I hang out with."

She regretted that last bit, but now that it was out there, she couldn't take it back.

"You mind holding that cigarette in your right hand?" he asked. "I know you're a lefty, but that smoke is making my eyes water."

"I had no idea you Texas boys were so sensitive," she said, transferring the cigarette to her non-dominant hand.

Cody turned on the radio, and they spent the remainder of the drive listening to a classic country station. Liza was more of a Journey girl, but she kept that to herself. She'd already insulted Cody once, and that was enough for one day.

He parked the Pinto in the employee lot of the Harper Technologies building. Liza unbuckled her seatbelt, opened the door, and was just about to slide out when she decided to invite Cody inside to meet Jonathan. Maybe the detective's presence would be enough to make Jonathan jealous. Not that Liza really wanted Jonathan in that way, but it seemed like a power move, the type of thing a cut throat businesswoman might do. And although she wasn't desperate for Jonathan's affection, she was desperate for his respect. She wanted him to see her as more than just a source of quick capital for his fledgling company. More than just a wallet with tits, in other words.

"Yeah, I don't suppose I have any other pressing engagements," Cody said as he twisted the ignition. The Pinto's engine coughed and sputtered as it shut down.

He followed her into the building. Since she could feel his eyes on her, she put a little extra oomph into her walk. She figured she owed him that much for driving her all the way out here.

The building was huge, but most of the offices were empty. Once business got started for real, the spaces would fill up fast. At least that was Jonathan's plan, anyway.

She led Cody up the central staircase and into Jonathan's oversized office, which looked more like the workspace of a nightclub manager than that of a computer technology CEO. Jonathan was on the far side of the room, using a putter to tap a golf ball toward an overturned coffee mug. The ball clunked into the cup, and Jonathan turned toward them, flashing his thousand watt smile.

"Liza, so good to see you," he said. His smile faded somewhat when he turned to Cody. "Hello there. I don't believe we've had the pleasure."

"Jonathan, this is Cody Abilene," Liza said. "He's a friend of my aunt who's staying with us for a few days."

The two men shook hands and shared a look that Liza recognized immediately. They were sizing one another up. She rolled her eyes. Any minute now, they'd be dropping their pants to have a pissing contest. Men were so predictable.

"Liza here was telling me that you're in computers," Cody said.

"Yes, that's correct." Jonathan nodded. "We're hardly IBM, but with some hard work and a bit of luck, we'll get there."

"That a fact?" Cody whistled softly. "I bet something like that really brings in the big bucks."

Jonathan nodded. "That's what our accountants tell me."

Liza cleared her throat, doing her best to insinuate herself between the two snarling dogs. She dug the envelope of cash out of her purse and passed it to Jonathan. "Speaking of investments, here's the funds we agreed upon. You said you had a new prospectus to show me, didn't you."

Jonathan stammered something unintelligible.

"Hard work, a bit of luck, and a hefty amount of investment capital. Nothing beats cold, hard cash, right?" Cody slapped Jonathan on the shoulder playfully. He was shorter than Jonathan by an inch or two, but he still seemed to be staring down at him.

"Well, yes, naturally…"

"I bet it's awful tempting to take money from some bad actors." Cody wasn't smiling anymore. "Like say, some Soviet spooks, for instance. I hear there's a lot of them sniffing around these small computer companies. You ever hear of anything like that?"

Suddenly, Liza had no idea what the hell was going on.

Jonathan regained enough composure to take her by the arm and maneuver her toward the conference room. He looked over his shoulder and gave Cody a parting shot. "I'm not sure I care for the implication, Mr. Abilene. Now, if you'll excuse us, we do have some important business to attend to. Some important legitimate and perfectly legal business, I might add."

"Fine, I'll just wait right here," Cody said.

Jonathan opened the door to the conference room. "That won't be necessary. I'll see that Liza gets home safely after our meeting is concluded."

Cody looked at her and raised his eyebrows questioningly.

"It's okay," she said. "I'll catch up with you back at Aunt Lillian's house, huh?"

"Guess I'll see myself out then." Cody looked at Jonathan, trying one more time to get a good read on the man. "Nice to meet you, Mr. Harper. Maybe we'll run into each other again someday."

"Yes, maybe someday…"

Cody left the office and made his way back through the building. The heels of his books clunked on the faux marble tile. He figured one good stomp could crack one of those tiles. Like so many things in the office—the leather furniture, the potted plants, the framed artwork on the walls—the floor was a fake. He wondered what that said about the place's owner.

He'd almost made it through the lobby when the three idiots spotted him on their way through the front door. Each of the three men was wide enough to necessitate opening both sides of the double door. Two of them were all muscle, while the third had girth that was hard won during his many trips through the buffet line. All three of them wore scowls like they were feeling either pissed off or dyspeptic. They paused as soon as they crossed the threshold, crossing their arms over their chest like bouncers and blocking the door.

"Well," Cody said, strolling across the lobby. "I recognize Tweedle Dee and Tweedle Dum, but I don't reckon I've ever seen your portly friend."

Tweedle Dee and Tweedle Dum were the two meatheads who'd stared Cody down during his last workout date with Bev McAfee. Now, here they were, staring him down again. Life was full of funny coincidences.

"Shut up, pipsqueak," the white meathead growled.

His buddy, the black guy with arms like tree trunks, blew Cody a kiss. "Yeah, pretty boy. I'd watch my mouth if I was you."

The third member of the gang just laughed, his jowly face quivering with each chuckle.

Cody shouldered past them and stepped out of the building. He put on his sunglasses and made his way to the Pinto, resisting the urge to glance over his shoulder to see if the trio of scowling morons were following him. He didn't need to be psychic to know that, sooner or later, they'd come at him. The threats might as well have been tattooed on their faces. Looked like he'd kicked the hornet's nest by needling Harper about possible connections to the Russians. Harper, just like compromised men throughout history, had taken it personally and overplayed his hand. If Cody suspected Harper of shady dealings before, he was convinced of it now.

To his great surprise, he was allowed to drive out of the parking lot unmolested. A few miles down the road, he was just starting to think that his private investigator's sixth sense might have given him a false alarm about the three stooges. But then he glanced at the rearview mirror and saw a black Town Car approaching at a high rate of speed.

"Well, shit," Cody muttered.

The Town Car got right up to his bumper before it swerved into the left lane and drew up alongside the Pinto.

"Well, if it ain't the three stooges coming back for an encore appearance," Cody sighed.

The fat one must have been the brains of the outfit. Or maybe he was just the spokesman. Either way, he was leaning half out of the passenger side window, frantically motioning for Cody to lower his window.

Cody did as requested, then shouted, "Hey, there. You boys lost?"

"Pull that piece of junk over," the fat man ordered. "Or else we'll put it the fuck over."

"That's no way to talk," Cody hollered back. "Now what would your mother think?"

Had he been in the DeLorean, he would have flipped them the bird, dropped the hammer down, and left those three imbeciles in the dust. As it was, he figured he might as well just pull over before they made good on the fat man's threat. The Town Car wasn't exactly Formula One material, but it could beat the Pinto no problem. Hell, a couple strong-legged dudes on a tandem bicycle could have given the Pinto a run for its money.

Cody took his foot off the gas and pulled onto the shoulder of the road. He turned off the engine, waited for the dust to settle, then got out. The three goons were already waiting on him.

"Name's Cody Abilene," Cody said, waving to them. "Pleased to make your acquaintance."

"I'm Matthew." The fat man jabbed himself in the chest with

his thumb. Then he gestured to his pals. "That mean looking white boy is Mark, and the even meaner looking brother is Luke. None of us is pleased to meet you."

"The Apostles, huh?" Cody shook his head. "But I bet you didn't ask me to pull over so you could invite me to the church picnic."

"You got that right," Luke growled. "We're here to fuck you up."

"Guys, come on," Cody said, peeling off his shirt and tossing it onto the Pinto's dusty hood. "You really don't want to mess with me. This body is a lethal weapon."

He did his best Schwarzenegger impression, flexing every muscle under his command. Mark and Luke must have thought the display was amusing. They did plenty of laughing as they removed their shirts. Thankfully, Matthew kept his Members Only jacket zipped up to his neck.

Now, while it was true the Apostles had Cody outgunned when it came to brute strength, he knew two things the apostles didn't know. The first was that Cody had spent the prior summer studying karate at Lee Kwan's Dojo of Honor. The second was that Cody had spent his childhood wrestling with his cousin Rowdy and was well versed in the art of fighting dirty. He demonstrated the first skill by landing a roundhouse kick to Luke's jaw, knocking the behemoth onto his ass. Then, Cody demonstrated the second skill set by kicking Mark in the balls. The big guy went down, clutching his family jewels and groaning like he felt seasick.

With the two big guys out of commission for the moment, Cody turned his attention to Matthew. The fat boy just stood there looking stupid as Cody swung a punch at his gut. Cody had expected it to feel like punching an oversized Jell-O mold. Instead, it felt like Matthew's gut was a slab of concrete.

Cody reeled, shaking his injured fist.

"Fucking dumbass," Matthew growled, unzipping his windbreaker to reveal a submachine gun strapped across his belly.

Luke and Mark had both recovered enough to stand upright. They each grabbed one of Cody's arms and held him in place while Matthew wriggled out of his jacket and unslung the machine gun. He stepped right up to Cody and pointed the barrel of the gun at Cody's crotch.

"How do you think you'd feel without a dick, Longhorn?" Matthew asked.

"Not too good, I reckon," Cody said. He wanted to add *But I bet your mom would feel even worse*, however this one a time when discretion was most certainly the better part of valor.

Cody must have not given them the answer they were looking for, because they all took turns giving him the punching bag treatment. Once they'd gotten it out of their systems, they dropped him on his ass so he could watch while Matthew took aim at the Pinto and emptied his gun's magazine. The first burst of bullets took out the Pinto's front grill. The engine vented steam like a geyser. A second burst blew the windshield to smithereens. After that, there was so much smoke and dust flying around that Cody couldn't keep track of the damage. One thing was for sure, the Pinto's best days were behind it.

Matthew took a second to admire his handiwork, then turned to Cody and said, "No more snooping around Mr. Harper's office, understand? We see you there again, it won't be a piece of shit car that gets shot up."

"Yeah," Mark said, giving Cody a kick for emphasis. "And stay away from Liza too. She's not your type."

"The fuck you talking about, man?" Luke elbowed his fellow apostle in the ribs. "What, you think she's gonna be your girlfriend or something? Gets old hearing you always talking about that chick."

"Shut up," Mark grunted. "I was just saying…"

"Put a fucking cork in it, both of you!" Matthew shouted. Then he smiled at Cody. "Remember what we talked about. Stay away from Mr. Harper. Now, hit the trail, buckaroo, before I change my mind about letting you walk away in one piece."

Chapter Seven

Cody didn't think they expected him to succumb to the elements. They wanted to scare him off, maybe even make him suffer a bit more in the bargain, but if they wanted him dead, they would have shot him and buried him out there in the desert. No, Cody told himself, they just wanted him to work up a thirst and get a sunburn to remember them by. Their boss probably figured killing him would spook Liza.

Luckily, they weren't out in the middle of nowhere, and Cody knew that a safe haven was only a couple miles away. Growing up on the racing circuit, you learned the location of just about every independent mechanic shop in every territory. If there was a spot where you could pick up after-market parts —stolen or legit—or maybe even get some modifications that weren't quite street legal, you became familiar with it. And that's how Cody knew exactly where to go: Tricky Rick's Used Cars. Rick Marshall went way back with Cody's dad, clear back to the days when Jimmy Dean Abilene was mowing down chumps like P.L. Buffington at racetracks across the nation on a weekly basis. Cody figured that a family friend, even one he hadn't seen in years, was his best shot at picking up some wheels without too much hassle.

The only problem was that Tricky Rick's Used Cars had been replaced by Ramona's Used Cars. Same dusty lot, same assortment of junkers and clunkers, but a different name on the sign out front. Still, it wasn't a total loss. Ramona Marshall was Rick's daughter, and it seemed as though she'd taken over the family business. Cody just hoped she remembered him well enough to give him a car on credit.

"Well, I guess you can't stop progress," Cody said to himself as he crossed the old state highway and onto the car lot.

He glanced around at the selection of cars on offer. It was a pretty sorry sight, but since beggars should never consider themselves choosers, he made the best of it. Surely, among the dozens of dusty vehicles, there was a car that could get him back to Bel Air without a blown radiator or thrown rod.

"See anything you like?"

The voice from behind Cody was a bit raspy, but it was unmistakably feminine. He took a deep breath and braced himself for the worst. He hadn't seen Ramona since they were both in third grade. Back then, she'd been a booger-picking, fart-lighting, gap-toothed tomboy who terrorized Cody and his brother. If she could, at the age of ten, out-cuss and out-fight a couple of West Texas boys, what sort of woman could she possibly have become in the intervening two decades? Probably some angry lesbian with jail house tattoos, someone who looked like Rick Marshall with tits.

He turned around slowly, expecting the worst. That deep breath he'd been holding whooshed out of him when he saw that the owner of that raspy voice was no monster. Far from it, in fact. Sure, there was a smudge of motor oil on her cheek and her hair was a mess of dusty tangles pulled into a haphazard ponytail, but otherwise, Ramona was pretty damn easy on the eyes. She sure as hell didn't resemble her father.

"Well?" she asked. "How about it? See anything you like?"

"I sure do." Cody cleared his throat. "I don't know if you remember me, but…"

"Of course I remember you, Cody Abilene. I just didn't expect to see you walk out of the desert, looking like you've just gotten your ass kicked. Don't tell me you're still picking fights by shooting off that smartass mouth of yours. Daddy always said your mouth would get you in trouble one of these days."

"Ol' Rick was a wise man," Cody said. "How is he these days?"

Ramona shook her head sadly. "He's been gone, let's see, almost ten years now."

"Damn, I hate to hear that Rick passed away. Seemed to me he was pretty close to indestructible."

"Passed away?" Ramona threw back her head and laughed. "Hell, I never said that! He's alive and well in Acapulco."

Now it was Cody's turn to laugh. "Say what?"

"After your family went back to Texas, daddy diversified his business interests. Moving stolen auto parts across the border from Mexico paid pretty well, but it paid even better when they were filled with marijuana. About ten years ago, he got into a bit of a tight spot with the DEA. When he felt the heat closing in, he hit the road with some cocktail waitress he met in Reno. Left me the business free and clear, then took off for Mexico. I get a postcard every now and then."

"Well, I'll be damned."

"Now you're not going to tell me that you got DEA agents breathing down your neck, are you? Because I only get to hang onto the family business as long as I keep my nose clean."

"Well now that you mention it, I am in a bit of trouble," Cody said. "But don't worry, I'm on the right side of the law."

He didn't have the energy to give her a detailed account of how he'd come to his current condition, so he gave her the highlights. He started from his fourth grade year, when his father had moved the family back to Texas, and worked his way up to his current career. She seemed suitably impressed when he told her about the case he was working.

"That's some story," she said. "But what do you need from me?"

"Girl, I need the fastest thing on this lot."

She smiled. At some point in the last couple decades, that gap between her front teeth had closed. Then she lowered the zipper of her coveralls, exposing a pair of perfectly formed breasts. Hard to believe this was the same girl who taught him how to ignite a fart with a Bic lighter. While Cody wasn't one to make quantitative judgments about the feminine form, he couldn't help thinking that the double handfuls staring him in the face were at least on par with June Khnockers' monumental assets. He whistled appreciatively.

"Honey," she said. "I'm the fastest thing on this lot."

"Oh, Lord have mercy." Despite his aches and pains, Cody felt himself rising to the occasion.

"I got to warn you..." She paused to stifle a laugh. "I drive a *hard* bargain."

"Then let's get into some deep negotiations." It wasn't Cody's best line, but his brain's blood supply was heading south, below the belt specifically.

"You still like to wrestle?" She grabbed his hand and led him toward the shop.

There was an El Camino in there. Its hood was raised and half the engine looked to have been removed, but there was a sleeping bag in the back. They climbed in and got reacquainted.

The fastest thing on Ramona's lot—at least the fastest thing she could part with for free—was a black Datsun Z. It had a few dents and dings, and the interior looked like the aftermath of a frat house gangbang, but Ramona had rebuilt the engine, so the car had it where it mattered most. It got him back to the Chamberlain estate in short order.

He parked in the driveway, right between the Bentley and

the Cadillac. The Datsun Z may have been a slight upgrade from the Pinto, but it still stuck out like a turd in a punchbowl.

But Cody didn't really give a shit about appearances. Despite Ramona's relaxing ministrations, he was still sore, both physically and emotionally, from the beating he'd taken at the hands of the apostles.

Enough pussyfooting around, he thought. *It's time for some honest-to-God investigating.*

A quick tour of the main house didn't turn up anything of interest. Stewart was in the entertainment room, listening to a Barbara Streisand record and dancing like a fool by himself. Lady Lillian was napping on the living room couch with her plaster-encased leg propped up on a pillow and a Danielle Steele paperback in her lap. Anita and Shane weren't in evidence, so Cody headed to the one place he thought they might be: Shane's place in the servants' quarters.

He bent low as he crept beneath the quarters' back window. Either the AC wasn't working or Shane and Anita just wanted a bit of fresh air, because the window had been raised a couple inches. Cody appreciated that. As a private investigator, he loved it when people made it easy to eavesdrop. He decided to press his luck and peaked through the gap between the window frame and the sill. He found himself staring at the backs of two heads full of sex-tousled hair. From the sound of things, Shane and Anita were enjoying the afterglow with a good old fashioned lovers' quarrel. They were seated on opposite ends of a small couch, glaring at one another.

"You know, it's a good thing God gave you that stick of dynamite in your boxer shorts," said Anita, "because he sure didn't give you brains. How stupid could you be, giving your scuzzy gambling friends this phone number?"

Shane responded like a scolded child pleading his case. "Look, it's no big deal. So I owe a guy some money. So what?"

"Shit like this makes me wonder if this thing hasn't run its course."

Cody inched up a little higher, trying to get a better view. Things inside the little house were heating up. He watched the butler slide across the couch and put his arm around Anita's shoulders.

"Come on, baby," Shane said. "Don't be cruel."

Anita shrugged his arm off. "To hell with you."

"Maybe it serve you right if some stuff got said about you. You might not feel so high and mighty if people got a look at your dirty laundry."

"What the hell are you even talking about?" Anita popped a stick of gum in her mouth and commenced chomping it with a vengeance. Cody was amazed that such delicate facial features could coexist with jaw muscles like that. She looked like she could grind a marble to dust between her molars.

Shane heaved himself up from the couch. Cody allowed himself a sigh of relief when he saw that the butler was only naked from the waist up.

"Oh, I don't know, Anita," said Shane, looming over her. "How about the story of the poor little rich girl getting it on with the hired help, who just happens to be an ex-con? That's the sort of thing that could end a marriage and get the wife written out of the family fortune. I mean, after all, the sort of shit that's been going on right under her queer hubby's turned-up faggot nose…"

Now we're getting to the good stuff, Cody thought as he watched Shane turn his back on Anita. The butler crossed the room and squatted in front of a cabinet, atop which stood a TV/VCR setup right out of some high-end electronics catalogue. He opened one of the cabinet drawers and pulled out a VHS tape, which he handled with all the reverence of a preacher showing off the family Bible.

"I got some state of the art video on you, baby," he said as he slotted the videocassette into the VCR and pressed Play.

Cody didn't have the best view of the TV, but he could see enough to get the gist of Shane's state of the art video. It wasn't the sort of thing with much plot. In Cody's experience, the best dirty movies never bother much with that stuff anyway. This particular dirty movie involved Shane and Anita going at it like a pair of jackrabbits in springtime. It was a hell of a thing to behold. Evidently, Anita was flexible enough that she could perform in a circus act if she ever fell on hard times.

"I also got some pictures you just gotta see," Shane said, pulling a manila envelope from the open drawer. He dumped the photos into his hand and flipped through them, commenting on them as he went. "Here's one with you on top. Oh, and this is one where you're doing that thing with your mouth. And this one has us doing that pose you got from that Hindu sex book…" He dropped the stack of photos on the couch. "Don't take my word for it. Have a look."

Anita came off the couch like she was spring-loaded and swung an open hand at Shane's face. Shane dodged the blow without much effort.

"You dirty bastard!" she shrieked, making a second attempt at a slap.

This time, Shane grabbed her hand. "Relax, baby. I wasn't going to show anyone. I just need you to understand how serious my situation is. And don't worry, your husband doesn't know about us as long as you help me out."

"Go to hell." She yanked her hand away. "I hope your scumbag bookie's thugs get ahold of you and tear you to pieces."

Cody barely had time to duck behind a nearby bush before Anita stormed out of the servants' quarters, slamming the door behind her.

"You goddamn whore!" Shane called after her.

Cody squatted behind the bush until he was sure the coast was clear, then headed back into the main house. After that show, he could use a drink to help him think things over. But that would have to wait. He had business to attend to.

First, he made a pit stop in his guest bedroom to retrieve an item from his supply of detective gadgets. This particular gadget was a listening device—a bug, in detective jargon—that he could listen to remotely through a pair of headphones. Whisper sensitive and so small it was easy to overlook, it was the latest in detective technology.

Now that he had the bug, it was time to plant it. Glancing over his shoulder to make sure he was unobserved, he went out to the circle drive in front of the house, where all the family's cars were parked. The Bentley was unlocked. For a group of people with so many secrets, the residents of the Chamberlain estate didn't seem to care about open windows and unlocked doors. That was fine with Cody. It made his job so much easier, especially when he needed to hide the bug beneath the Bentley's dashboard.

Chapter Eight

After another uncomfortable family dinner—lobster bisque and roast squab with lemon couscous and asparagus this time—the members of the family scattered. Stewart and Anita retired to their bedroom. Liza went to the game room to ping away at one of the three pinball machines. Lady Lillian rolled her wheelchair to the TV room just in time to catch a *Magnum P.I.* rerun. Shane and Marian busied themselves with their domestic duties. By all outward appearances, it was a normal family evening. If Cody didn't know better, he'd have thought they were normal, well-adjusted folks just going about their routines. Funny how appearances could lie.

He watched a couple reruns with Lady Lillian and made small talk, then excused himself to his bedroom. After a suitable interval, he killed the lights so it would look like he was going to bed. Then he popped his headphones onto his ears and listened to Molly Hatchet while he waited for the bug to cut in with any activity. He had a hunch that Shane wouldn't hang around all night twiddling his thumbs, and it didn't take long for that hunch to pay off. Around 11 p.m., he heard a flurry of activity in the Bentley. From the sound of things, Stewart was catching a ride into the city with Shane playing chauffeur.

Cody smiled to himself as he crept through the house. Now he was getting down to some real detective work, by God.

The game is afoot, he thought.

Although Cody gave Shane an overly cautious lead, the Bentley wasn't hard to follow. Shane was a lot of things, but a reckless driver wasn't one of them. And even in Hollywood, a car like that stuck out like a sore thumb.

Cody was pretty well-versed in Sunset Strip watering holes, but he didn't recognize the one that Shane parked in front of. Its narrow doorway was tucked away between two larger establishments. Maybe it was one of those exclusive speakeasy places Cody had read about in last month's issue of *Experience LA*. According to the pink neon sign, the bar in question was called The Screaming Cockatoo Club. The people trickling in and out of the place made it clear what sort of demographic the club catered to. The clientele were dressed to the nines in style that could only be described as absolutely, flamboyantly fabulous. It looked like a gay pride parade might kick off on the sidewalk outside the club. Not that Cody cared about that stuff. He was an open-minded man of the world with a strong belief in the "live and let live" philosophy. He even owned a copy of Cyndi Lauper's *She's So Unusual* record.

He went parked alongside the street a few spaces behind the Bentley, then killed the Datsun's engine and settled his headphones onto his ears. He made a mental note to pass along his regards to Marv at the electronics store. The voices in the headphones came through crystal clear, even over the noise of the Bentley's idling engine and the passing traffic.

"This goddamn fruit basket joint again," Shane grumbled. "You know how those TV preachers are always saying that God is gonna smite the Sodomites? Looking at the freaks in this place, I almost believe it."

"Well, now I've heard it all," Stewart snapped. "An ex-con delivering a lecture on morals. That's rich, especially coming from you. And you know exactly what I'm talking about."

Cody had to give it to Stewart. The little dude wasn't letting Shane intimidate him.

"You know," Shane said, "you keep up these performances at this place, word's bound to get out."

"I guess I'll just take my chances, honey," Stewart replied.

"You have a better chance of playing queen of the night if you help me out. For thirty grand, I can see to it that your secret stays hidden. You should consider it. Thirty large is nothing to a rich boy like you."

Stewart laughed. "Blackmail is blackmail, sweetheart, no matter the price tag."

"In that case, have a look at these pictures." There was the sound of rustling papers, then Shane continued, "Those would look great in the next issue of the Faggot Gazette. In case you're wondering, that's you on the bottom, sweets. I gotta say, you really took it like a champ. Now, if you can get me that cash by Lady Lillian's charity fundraiser, maybe these photos remain our little secret."

Not much shocked Cody these days, but he had to admit that he didn't figure Shane for a switch hitter. Must have been a trick he picked up in the joint. Or maybe not. Could be that was just the way he was wired.

"Even if I took your threats seriously, which I don't, that doesn't give me much time to come up with the cash." If Stewart was at all afraid, his voice didn't sound like it. "But I'm not going to keep you in suspense. The answer is still no."

Cody's bug picked up the soft *thunk-thunk* of the Bentley's rear door opening. He retrieved his binoculars from the passenger seat and focused them on the figure who climbed out of the car. Cody couldn't believe his eyes. Stewart emerged from the Bentley wearing an evening gown, a blonde wig, and an impressive set of fake boobs. Even through the high-resolution lenses of Cody's binoculars, the transformation from skinny pipsqueak to gorgeous woman was stunning. If Cody didn't know better, he would have been entirely fooled, and he wasn't too proud to admit it.

His headphones played the sound of Shane muttering, "Goddamn faggots."

Then the Bentley pulled back into the stream of traffic.

Cody could only shake his head. This case just kept getting better and better. He grabbed his mini tape recorder off the passenger seat and hit Record.

"Well, my investigation rolls on," he said. "And the hits just keep on coming. Let me tell you about what I saw tonight at a hip little joint called The Screaming Cockatoo Club..."

The next day was quiet. Cody spent the morning soaking his sore body in the backyard hot tub. Liza joined him for a while. She spent the entire time chattering about inane rich girl bullshit. Lots of talk about shopping and the new restaurants she'd visited.

"And there's this place called The Square Peg that serves sushi pizza," she said. "Have you ever heard of something so cool? And my friend Angela knows the sous chef, so we got a table, even though the restaurant is booked solid for a month. After that, we ran into Jennifer and her new boyfriend at the record store..."

Cody tried to follow along, but gave up after five minutes. He wondered if Liza ever paused to take a breath. He also wondered if she knew anything about his little dust-up with Jonathan Harper's thugs, the Apostles. The fact that she didn't once mention Cody's split-open eyebrow or the bruises on his ribs spoke volumes. He had to admit, her indifference stung him. In fact, he was so stunned that he gave her a taste of her own medicine. When she casually shed her bikini top and stretched her arms over her head so that her nipples peeked above the hot tub's waterline, Cody pretended to yawn. She must have taken the hint, because she got out of the water a few minutes later.

Since he'd had enough of rich people food, he took the afternoon off and drove into town for a burrito and a beer at El Coyote. What the hell, he figured. After all the hours he'd put in yesterday, he deserved a couple hours to himself.

Once he'd put away his fill of Mexican food, he burned off some of the calories by walking to the Rainbow Bar and Grill. He took a seat at the bar so he could replace those calories with a cold beer or two. He'd just taken his first sip of Budweiser when a friend strolled through the door.

"Well, if it isn't my favorite member of the royal class," he said as Contessa Luciana De Rossi perched on the stool next to his. "Imagine seeing you in a place like this. If I didn't know better, I'd think you were keeping tabs on me."

She asked the bartender for a white wine spritzer then turned to Cody. She asked him how the case was progressing.

"I didn't know I was expected to give progress reports," he said. "But I can tell you that your friend Lady Chamberlain has a regular soap opera unfolding under her roof. Now suppose you tell me what brings you around? I thought you split town after we had our night on the town. In case you were wondering, I wasn't insulted by your quick disappearance."

"I caught a flight out of Heathrow yesterday," she explained. "I never miss one of Lady Lillian's charity events. I assume you will be in attendance. You have evening wear, yes? These events are strictly black tie."

"I'm more of a blue jeans type of guy, but I suppose I can throw something together."

The Contessa laughed like he'd just told a real knee-slapper. "This round of drinks is on me. After that, we're going to visit my friend Martino's store and get you suitable clothes. If you're going to be my date, you better look the part."

"I wish getting a date to senior prom had been this easy," he said. "Gina Lockhart made me buy her dinner *and* flowers."

Lady Lillian Chamberlain's little soiree was supposed to raise money for starving children in Africa, but Cody figured the party, like most similar events, was an excuse for a bunch of rich folks to gather and show off to one another. There certainly were plenty of them circulating through the house's first floor rooms. The champagne flowed freely, there was no shortage of fancy hors d'oeuvres, and a trio of bored-looking jazz musicians were set up in one corner, working their way through a selection of soft melodies.

As far as the guest list went, it was quite a collection of characters. In one room alone, he recognized several aging actresses, two professional golfers, and a half dozen runway models hanging on the arms of their geriatric millionaire husbands. Cody would have felt out of place if not for the fact that his date was a genuine Contessa who also happened to have a beautiful face and a body that belonged on a magazine cover. Her evening ensemble put that body on display to such a degree that Cody was certain it caused a minor scandal among the upper class partygoers. The top of her dress was no more than two crisscrossed strips of fabric that barely kept her breasts in check. The dress may have been ankle-length, but it was slit on both sides right up to the tops of her thighs. She damn sure wasn't wearing a bra and Cody would have bet the contents of his wallet that her panties were also MIA.

They were stationed in the corner, sipping expensive champagne, when she asked him if he'd noticed Jonathan Harper chatting up Lady Chamberlain throughout the evening.

"Yeah, I've been watching him slime his way around the room," Cody said. "Angling for investments at a charity event. I may be a simple country boy, but I know that's in bad taste."

"Lady Lillian is convinced his interest in Liza goes beyond the financial," said Luciana. "It's probably just wishful thinking on her part, wanting to see her niece married to a successful businessman. Hopefully, Liza keeps things strictly professional, because from what you told me earlier today, it sounds like Harper's mixed up in something."

"He's suspect *numero uno* if you ask me."

Shane the butler was circulating through the crowd, collecting empty glasses. He paused in front of them and greeted Luciana by name while accepting their empties.

"That dude's a snake," Cody said as Shane continued on his slow circuit of the room.

"There's more than one snake at this party," Luciana replied. "Take a look around."

Cody did as she suggested. In one corner, Marian the maid was giggling with a couple of Jonathan Harper's cronies. They looked awfully familiar. Stewart and Anita were perched on a couch, doing their best to look like they enjoyed each other's presence. Anita had certainly taken advantage of the free-flowing champagne. Her laughter was frequent and a couple notches louder than what was probably considered polite for such a gathering.

Shane had been drawn into a heated discussion with a couple of heavy-looking dudes wearing Rolex watches and diamond pinkie rings. Whatever they were discussing must have been exciting. All three of them were punctuating their words with emphatic gestures.

Luciana nodded in their direction. "Any clue what that's about?"

"Oh, I have a pretty good idea," Cody said. "Shane is, among other things, a serious gambler. And not a very good one either. He owes money to more than one bookie. I had to guess, I'd say that those two old boys are doing their best to collect on one of those bookies' behalf."

"Shocking," Luciana said, although her tone of voice contradicted her words.

"Like I said, it's a regular soap opera in this house," Cody laughed.

"Quite," Luciana agreed.

Shane had done his best to keep his voice down when he was forced to speak to Vic Santino. That wasn't a problem. Venomous Vic wasn't a man who needed to raise his voice to make a point. His reputation spoke much louder than words. Every serious gambler in the state had heard stories about the man. Any number of those stories could be the inspiration for a horror movie.

If Shane had known that Top Shelf Catering was one of the Santino family's businesses, he would have steered Lady Lillian towards another company. But it was too late for that now. Vic himself had shown up under the guise of supervising his employees, but he'd really come to tell Shane that it was way past time that he squared his gambling debts. The way Vic stared at him while he was trying to do his job was starting to get to Shane. He could feel those eyes boring holes right through him. And those two goons kept cracking their knuckles and flashing shark-teeth smiles his way, like they'd just stepped out of some gangster movie.

Shane grabbed Marion by the arm and guided her into the kitchen. He dumped his tray of empty champagne glasses into the sink full of soapy water and pulled her in close.

"Listen, honey," he said. "I gotta disappear for a little while. Can you cover for me?"

Marian tossed her head, stirring her rat's nest of waist-length hair. She rolled her eyes so dramatically that Shane was afraid they might get stuck that way.

"But it's so busy out there," she whined. "The guys from the catering company are barely helping me. All they want to do is pinch my butt when I walk by. One of them even groped my tits when no one was looking."

Despite the situation, Shane almost laughed. Marian was a weirdo with the world's worst hairdo, but even with those two strikes against her, she was still a nice piece of ass. She certainly lived up to the old stereotypes about crazy broads being dynamite in the sack.

"I'll make it up to you later, I promise," he begged. "I'll do that thing you like for as long as you want."

"You mean that thing you learned in France?"

Shane nodded. He'd actually learned the trick in question from a guy in the joint, but she didn't need to know that.

Marian considered the offer for a moment then nodded. "Okay, but just remember you said I could have it for as long as I want."

"I'll learn to breathe through my ears if I have to," he promised.

"Well, you better get going," she said.

He gave her a quick kiss then disappeared out the back door. He hit the ground running and headed for the servants' house. His thoughts were racing, and his pulse was doing its best to keep up. By the time he fumbled his keys out of his pocket and let himself into his little house, he was damn near hyperventilating. He shed his jacket and collapsed on the couch, tugging at his bowtie. It took him a minute to calm himself down, then he grabbed the phone and dialed.

Marian answered on the fifth ring. Her voice dripping exasperation, she said, "Chamberlain Estate. How can I help you?"

He did his best to disguise his voice when he told her that he had an urgent matter to discuss with Stewart Chamberlain.

"Tell him it's his friend Frederick calling," Shane said, trying to imitate the lisping delivery of Stewart's main butt-buddy.

"Hang on a sec," Marian replied.

Shane stretched the phone cord to its limit so he could grab a

Coke from the fridge. The last thing he needed was caffeine, but damn it, he was thirsty.

"Frederick, honey, where are you?" Stewart sounded breathless with excitement. "I thought you were going to come to the party."

"This is Shane, you faggot," Shane growled. "The time has come for you to give me that money or I'll plaster those photos all over town. You know what I'm saying? Your wife is going to know exactly how you get your kicks."

Stewart laughed. Shane couldn't believe it. The little cocksucker actually laughed.

"Shane, honey, I told you last night the answer was no. And I don't give a damn if show your little pictures to Anita. It's nothing she doesn't already know. We have an understanding, you see. Now kindly fuck off."

The line went dead. Shane slammed the receiver back onto its cradle so hard that the bell dinged. No wonder Anita was so brazen about sneaking off to the beach house with him whenever she got the itch. Why should she give a shit if her husband was a queer if it meant she could play around however she chose? Shane cursed himself for missing it. All that wasted effort...

The walls were closing in on him.. He tried not to panic as he forced himself to think of some way to get his hands on thirty grand quick.

He came up with exactly jack shit. And then, because no matter how bad things seem, they can always get worse, the door to the servants' quarters burst open with enough force that the doorknob dented the drywall. Standing there, silhouetted by moonlight, was Venomous Vic himself. The gun in his right hand looked like the kind that could put a fist-sized hole through a man's body. Shane sat on the couch, frozen by fear. It didn't matter that he could probably take Vic in a straight-up fight. If he so much as laid a finger on a member of the Santino family, he'd be signing his death warrant. Whatever Vic had in mind, Shane knew he had to sit there and take it. His only hope was that Vic remembered that a dead man couldn't pay his debts.

"I am at the end of my rope with you," Vic growled. "You hear me, you piece of shit? I'm fresh out of patience. I'm giving you exactly forty-eight hours to make good on what you owe. You don't pay up, I'm going to have you fed to my father's pet tiger. Now open your mouth."

"No, you gotta understand…" Shane sputtered.

"Open up, tough guy, or I'll knock those pearly whites out of your fucking mouth."

Shane did as he was told. Vic stepped closer and put the gun in his mouth. Shane nearly gagged at the oily, metallic taste. His throat worked convulsively, his Adam's apple bobbing up and down in his neck like it was trying to escape.

"I want you to remember how this tastes, Shane. Because the next time this flavor hits your tongue, it'll be the last thing you taste." Vic yanked the gun back, chipping one of Shane's incisors in the process. "Forty eight hours, asshole."

Shane didn't know if it was fear or relief that nearly made him piss himself as Vic walked out of the servants' quarters. He stumbled into the bathroom and did his business. After he flushed, he checked his teeth in the mirror. The chipped tooth wasn't that bad. All things considered, it was a small price to pay if it got Vic off his back. He splashed some cold water on his face. Some time to think, that's all he needed. He'd been in tight spots before and managed to escape with his life and all his parts intact. As long as he didn't freak out, he could do it again.

There was no problem so big or complicated that it didn't have a solution.

First things first, he had to get back to the party. If he was gone much longer, that goddamn Cody Abilene might start getting suspicious. He'd already been giving Shane the stink eye for most of the night. No telling what sort of damage he could do if he started poking into Shane's business.

He struggled with the bow tie but eventually got it back on. He gave himself one more look in the mirror then headed back to the party. Queen Stewart practically pounced on him as soon as he got back to work.

"Shane, I was beginning to think you'd run out on us," he chirped. "Be a dear and fetch me another glass of champagne. I'm positively parched."

"Faggot," Shane muttered under his breath as took Stewart's empty glass.

At least Vic seemed to have called it a night. He and his goons were nowhere to be found. There were still plenty of rich assholes to deal with, but at least none of them could have him killed with a snap of their fingers. And so what if that cowboy private investigator kept looking at him? That lucky bastard was going to have his hands full with the Contessa the rest of the night. She looked like the type who knew every trick in the book. Had Shane not been juggling so many problems at once, he might have taken a run at her himself. Plenty of these rich broads got a charge out of slumming it with the help, after all.

Sometime after midnight, the party started to wind down. An hour later, it was in its death throes, with the last few guests streaming out the front door. As predicted, the Contessa disappeared upstairs with the cowboy detective. Stewart and Anita retired to their room to... do whatever it was they did when they were alone. Finally, Shane carried Lady Lillian up the stairs to her bedroom with Marian following close behind. He said his goodnights and beat a hasty retreat, leaving Marian to deal with Lady Lillian's bedtime routine.

The door to the servants' quarters was open when he got there. Vic had busted the lock when he'd kicked it open earlier. Shane would have to fix it, of course, but that could wait until the morning. All he had the energy for at the moment was sitting on the couch and drinking a beer before getting in bed. He didn't even have enough left in the take for a shower. And he didn't know what the hell he'd do if Marian came looking to collect on her payment for covering his absence during the party. Just in case, he put a tape in the VCR. It was the tape of him and Anita fucking their brains out. Watching it was a last ditch effort to get himself excited. Maybe he could get it up for Marian, after all.

He shrugged off his jacket, unknotted his tie, and popped the top on a cold Miller Lite. That first foamy mouthful was like manna from heaven. It had been one long fucking night. He practically melted into the couch.

A few minutes later, there was a knock at the door. Shane sighed. Marian must have just dumped the old lady in bed and raced down here. Under normal circumstances, that would be just peachy. Marian might have been a few donuts shy of a baker's dozen, and yeah, that hair could have been classified as a felony in some jurisdictions, but she was fun in the sack. She was easy to please and screamed like she was being murdered when she got off. And hell, watching the homemade porno tape with her might be fun. Marian was usually up for the kinky shit.

"Just a second," he called as there was another, more insistent knock. The hinges squeaked as the door opened. Then the sound of two soft footfalls. "Don't worry, baby. I got what you need. You feel like watching a dirty movie with me?"

No response.

"Okay, we don't have to watch it," he said. "You don't got to be bitchy about it."

He took a deep breath and heaved himself off the couch...

...and found himself staring at a shadowy figure wearing a trench coat. He stepped closer to get a better look at the person who'd just entered the room. The figure wore black gloves, and there was a switchblade clutched in one hand. He stepped closer and leaned forward to get a look at the intruder's face.

"Oh, it's you..."

That was all he managed to get out before the knife plunged into his stomach. The trench coat-clad figure tugged the knife free, drew it back, and stabbed again. Pain sheared through Shane's guts as the knife twisted cruelly before the intruder tugged it free again. Blood spurted from the wound. His head felt like a helium balloon trying to pull free from his body. He staggered a couple aimless steps then collapsed to the floor.

The intruder stepped over him and ripped the videocassette out the VCR, then slipped it into the coat's inside pocket. Shane waited until the intruder was headed for the door before he made his move. Getting to his feet took Herculean effort, but he managed it. He took two shuffling steps forward, fighting hard to keep his equilibrium, and opened the drawer beneath the TV. A few of his best cameras were in there, and he grabbed the first one he touched. He turned around and snapped two off-balance shots of the intruder. In the darkened room, the flash was light a lightning bolt.

"Gotcha," he whispered, tossing the camera back into the drawer.

He fumbled the key to the drawer out of his pocket. The strength went out of his legs, and he hit the ground. His vision was starting to blur, and the world seemed to go all wobbly around him. Still he managed to lock the drawer before collapsing on to his back. He worked the key loose from the key ring, then popped it into his mouth and swallowed it. The metal tore at his throat, but he got it down without gagging. He could feel it scraping his innards on the way down.

The intruder pulled a gun—a big-ass Dirty Harry pistol with a silencer attached to the barrel—and fired two shots in quick succession into Shane's chest. The impact was like Godzilla stomping on him.

The last thing Shane saw before taking a long plunge into darkness was the intruder using the knife to jimmy the drawer open. He rolled onto his belly, sending a fresh wave of agony through his body. The pain forced him into a strange clarity. He crawled forward, slipping in puddles of his own blood. The door was so close. Once he made it outside… well, he hadn't thought that far ahead. He grunted, summoning every bit of strength he had left to drag himself through the doorway. He was halfway through when another bullet punched through his spine. He coughed up a mouthful of blood then collapsed face down in it.

Oh, well, he thought. *Guess it was worth a try…*

And that was it.

Chapter Nine

Cody and Luciana lingered in bed for a while. Usually, Cody popped right out of bed in the morning, eager to face the day. But for some reason, he felt groggy. Maybe the Contessa had sapped all his strength with her style vigorous lovemaking. The last thing he remembered was collapsing onto the sweat-damp sheets while she fetched him a glass of water. So they slept until a fashionably late hour then went for a morning swim. They were enjoying a late poolside breakfast of Eggs Benedict and fresh tropical fruit when they found Shane's body.

They were seated poolside, their bathing suits still dripping. As they sipped mimosas and enjoyed the morning breeze, a gentle but insistent thumping noise caught Cody's ear.

"You hear that?" he asked. "Sounds like it's coming from over there."

He pointed to the tall hedgerow that separated the pool from the small house that served as the servants' quarters.

"No, I don't hear…" Luciana cocked her head to one side. "Yes, I believe I do hear something."

It didn't take them long to track down the source of the noise. The front door of the servants' quarters was open, and the breeze was pushing it around. Just when the door started to drift closed, the breeze would kick up and push it back. It would thump against the outside wall then begin its slow rebound before being swept back by the breeze again. There was a good reason the door could never fully close. Laid out across the threshold, like the world's nastiest doorstop, was Shane the butler's dead body.

"Well, there's something you don't see every day," Cody said.

"My God," said Luciana, peering into the small house. "It looks like he was trying to drag himself to safety. There's a great deal of blood in there."

"Yeah, I bet. From the looks of things, he took a few bullets." Cody took the Contessa by the elbow and pulled her away from the body. "Look, Luciana, you need to get away from here. You said you have a flight back to Italy tonight. Any chance you can catch an earlier flight? Because this place is gonna be crawling with cops in short order. You don't need to get mixed up in that investigation. If your name comes up, I'm your alibi. We were together all night. But right now, you need to put some distance between yourself and this mess."

She shook her head. "But I'm worried about you. I'd rather stay here."

"Hell, this is nothing I can't handle. My middle name is Danger."

"Your middle name is James."

"Well, daddy thought Danger had a good ring, but mama had other ideas. Still, I can handle things on this end. No sense getting your family name dragged through the mud if we can avoid it."

"I guess you're right," she sighed. "Promise me you'll take care of yourself."

Cody leaned in for a one last kiss, then sent her on her way. He looked down at Shane's lifeless body. Someone had really done a number on the old boy. Whatever the motive was, one thing was clear: this had been personal.

"The plot thickens," Cody sighed.

There was no way to avoid police involvement now, no matter how much Lady Lillian wanted to keep the family name out of the papers. But first things first, Cody decided. He needed to put on some clothes. There are some things a man can comfortably do while wearing nothing but a bright red Speedo. Facing a bunch of cops at a murder scene wasn't one of them.

Cody put on his cleanest pair of jeans and a comfortable shirt. He also slipped his holster to his belt and covered it with his shirttail. It was his considered opinion that once the investigation took a turn for murder, it was time to arm yourself. Better safe than sorry when a killer was lurking around. Once he'd run a comb through his hair and squirted on a bit of cologne, he headed back to the servants' quarters. He wanted to take one last look around before the calling the cops. Once they arrived and the yellow crime scene tape went up, they wouldn't allow him to set foot in Shane's quarters until they'd finished going over it with a fine toothed comb. That could take the better part of the day. Cody didn't think it was in his client's best interest that he remain idle for that long.

He stepped carefully over Shane's body and slid into the house. Once inside, he saw that he wasn't the only one investigating the crime scene. Anita was across the room, rifling through the contents of a drawer below the TV stand.

"Anita? What are you doing here?" he asked.

She looked like a kid who'd been caught trying to sneak a candy bar out of the drug store without paying for it. She stammered out an excuse. "I was just walking by the servants' quarters and saw Shane's body. I came in here to... I don't know why actually... I guess I'm just in shock. I mean, this is horrible..."

Cody wasn't buying it. She was up to something. But now wasn't the time to call her on her bullshit. He told her to go gather the members of the family and have them meet by the pool in ten minutes. Once she'd run back to the main house, he had a look at those drawers she'd been so interested in. It was immediately apparent that someone—the killer, most likely—had jimmied the drawers open. There were gouges in the wood on the right side of the lock. There was a bit of blood too. Could have been that the killer nicked a finger while trying to use a knife to pry the drawer open. Or maybe it was some of Shane's blood. Cody wasn't equipped for that sort of forensic investigation.

What the hell were you doing in here, Anita? he wondered.

He figured the most likely answer was that Anita was poking around, trying to find those photos of Shane giving her the business. If that was indeed where Shane had kept them, they were gone now. All that remained was a few nudie magazines, a dime bag of weed, some racing forms, a dog-eared book on strategies for becoming a better poker player, a tube of personal lubricant, a half-eaten Snickers bar, and a camera smudged with dark globs of dried blood.

"Well, what have we here?" Cody said, lifting the camera out of the drawer.

He was no photography expert, but he could tell that whoever had been using the camera had come to the end of the roll of film. He popped the camera's back panel open and took out the film roll. Sure, it could be considered withholding evidence, but Cody wanted to get a look at whatever was on that film. If he handed it over to the cops right away, he'd never get a chance, and he would have bet the contents of his wallet that whatever evidence was on that film was central to his investigation. Call it detective's intuition or simple gut instinct. He pocketed the film then closed the drawers, using the edge of his shirt to make sure he didn't leave any fingerprints on the handles.

Stepping out of that little house of horrors was a relief. It looked like it was going to be the sort of sunny day that only existed in southern California. The air smelled of flowers and cut grass. The birds in the trees were singing their songs. The breeze was soft and carried the promise of a day filled with excitement. You'd hardly guess that there was a grisly murder scene just a few feet away. That was how it went, Cody supposed.

When he got back to the swimming pool, the family was seated at the large picnic table. He didn't need to ask if Anita had filled them in on the reason for the hastily assembled meeting. Their expressions made it abundantly clear that they knew the score.

Lady Lillian was the first to speak up. Before Cody could even get a word out, she said, "Oh, Cody, this is a terrible thing. Just terrible. Shane had his faults, but he was a good driver and so handy around the house."

Stewart chimed in next. "I don't know why, but I can't help feeling this is somehow my fault. It's just… well, it's a tragedy."

Cody wondered what the hell Stewart was talking about. "Well, Stewart, I wouldn't suggest saying that stuff when the police get here. They might take it the wrong way."

"No, you don't understand," Stewart said. "I was the one who hired him."

Anita and Lillian murmured something about how Stewart shouldn't beat himself up about it. Stewart studied the sun-dappled surface of the pool water. He nodded slowly.

"Now, if y'all will excuse me," Cody told the family, "I need to make a phone call."

There was a phone on the outside wall of the pool cabana. He supposed it was mostly used to call the line in the main house when the drinks and snacks ran low. Maybe, if there was a party going on, it was used to order a pizza. Did rich people have pizzas delivered? Cody wasn't certain. He felt like every class of people loved pizza, but you never knew with rich folks. But today that phone wasn't needed to order a fresh pitcher of

Margaritas or to give Domino's a holler. It was needed for more urgent business.

He grabbed the receiver off the wall and dialed his answering service. Since Cody was just a working stiff, he couldn't afford a one of those fancy services, much less a private secretary, so he had to make do with a less conventional method. His friend Sally ran a phone sex service out of a tiny office in Burbank. For a few bucks a month—a cost Cody offset with more intimate forms of payment—Sally moonlighted as his answering service. Cody liked to think of it as a creative solution to one of life's little problems. Plus, Sally was a hell of a lot of fun.

She answered after one ring. "Hello, caller, this is Sexy Sally on the line, ready to satisfy your steamiest fantasies."

Despite the situation, Cody couldn't help but smile. "Hey there, Sal, this is Cody Abilene. You got anything for me?"

"Oh, Cody, you sexy cowboy…" Sally moaned in her best phone sex voice. "I wish I could have your manhood pressing against me right now…"

"Yeah, Sally, sounds great." Cody glanced over at the Chamberlain family. They were staring back at him with expectant looks on their faces. The pool cabana was only about ten feet from where they sat. At least they were out of earshot.

"I'm serious, Cody. I want to feel you inside me." Sally was really turning up the heat. "My nipples are hard just thinking about it…"

Cody turned his back on the family so they couldn't see the redness he felt creeping into his cheeks. "Gonna have to take a rain check on that, sweetheart. Right now, I need you to call the police. Ask for Sergeant Beverly McAfee. Tell her that there's been a homicide at the Chamberlain estate. Tell her Cody says to keep a lid on it as best she can. Really emphasize the need for discretion. You got all that?"

Sally sighed. The next time she spoke, she'd dropped the phone sex act. "Sure thing, Cody. Oh, and while I've got you on the line, you've had about a dozen calls from a girl named Faye and another dozen from a girl named May. All they'll say is that they miss you."

"Good Lord, how did they even get your number?"

"I guess you're just so good that a woman will go to any length to track you down," Sally laughed. "Maybe someday soon you can give me a reminder of how good you are."

"We'll have to schedule that for a later date. I gotta run, sweetheart." He hung up the phone and went back to the family. He sat on the edge of a chaise lounge and told them the police would be along any minute.

"I do hope they'll be discreet," Lady Lillian said. "I'd hate to see the family name mixed up in some sort of scandal."

Cody assured her that Bev would be discreet. "Don't you worry. Bev will keep a lid on this thing. She and I go way back."

Unfortunately, the police response didn't live up to Cody's reassurances. Sergeant Beverly McAfee showed up in an unmarked car, but that was the end of the discreet portion of the investigation. That unmarked car was at the head of a procession of law enforcement vehicles, including three squad cars, a medical examiner van, a morgue wagon, and a crime scene unit van.

Well, Cody thought, *at least they didn't have the lights and sirens going.*

He trotted through the main house and met Bev at the front door before she had a chance to ring the bell. She was looking sexy as ever, despite her all-business posture. But she wasn't alone on the doorstep. Lieutenant Arledge had come with her. His characteristically stony expression could have allowed him to bluff his way through a Vegas poker tournament. He was an old school detective and he certainly looked the part in his dark suit and matching fedora.

"Lieutenant," Cody said, offering his hand to shake. "Gotta say I'm surprised to see you here. Or is the department mandating a lieutenant on scene for every homicide?"

"God, no." Arledge shook his head. "In this city, we'd have to promote like crazy to have enough lieutenants to keep up. No, I'm afraid this case has grown legs. Take me to the family and I'll explain."

"Right this way," Cody said, leading them through the house.

Arledge whistled appreciatively at the furnishings and décor. "I knew I should have gone into plastics instead of law enforcement."

Cody led them out to the back patio and through the gate to the swimming pool. He presented the two officers to the family. "I'd like you to meet Sergeant McAfee and Lieutenant Arledge. They'll be handling this case personally."

"Nice to meet you," Lady Lillian said. "I wish it could be under better circumstances."

Bev smiled and spoke a few of the usual pleasantries, but the lieutenant got right down to business. He passed Lady Lillian a manila envelope.

"Lady Chamberlain, this arrived at my office this morning," the lieutenant explained. "Imagine my surprise to see it addressed to you. Of course, it all made better sense once Sergeant McAfee received that call from Mr. Abilene's..." He paused and gave Cody a disappointed frown, then continued, "From his rather unconventional answering service."

Bev clapped a hand over her mouth to stifle laughter. Cody wondered just what the hell Sally had said on that phone call to the police precinct. Knowing Sally, it probably involved handcuffs and/or nightsticks being used for unintended purposes.

Lady Lillian opened the envelope and took out a stack of photos. As she flipped through them, her eyes grew wider and wider. "Anita, how could you? These photos are of you and Shane doing... unmentionable acts."

Cody peered over her shoulder and gave the photos a glance. "Nice composition. A little out of focus, but I guess you can't have everything."

Anita sputtered, failing to come up with any plausible excuse. Cody wondered if the gears of her brain had completely locked up. He almost expected smoke to pour out of her ears. To his credit, Stewart took the news in stride. His expression didn't falter one bit.

Lady Lillian stuffed the photos back in the envelope and handed them back to Arledge.

The lieutenant came close to breaking a smile when he said, "Now this is what we call hard evidence."

If Lady Lillian heard the remark, she didn't dignify it with a response. Instead, she turned her withering glare on her daughter-in-law. "Those awful photos were taken at the family beach house. How could you, Anita?"

Anita stared intently at the clear water of the swimming pool like it might offer some convenient escape route. She certainly didn't make eye contact with Lady Lillian.

Bev cleared her throat. "I don't suppose you have a key to this beach house handy, do you?"

⤴

Marian Hayward had gotten her fill of the Chamberlain family. She was already leaning towards giving up her gig as the family's maid and trying her luck at one of the resorts south of the border. Now that Shane had been murdered, her mind was made up. There were bad vibes at the estate. Real bad vibes. Marian was a Pisces, so she was especially sensitive to that sort of thing.

But as much as she wanted to throw her possessions—some clothes, a few crystals, a deck of tarot cards, and an astounding collection of hair care products—into a suitcase and hit the road, she still have some loose ends to tie up. Her obligations to

Jonathan Harper weren't the sort of thing she could skip out on. If she did, she'd spend her days at the Mexican resort looking over her shoulder. That man wasn't the type to just let things go. Marian had heard stories.

She didn't have a phone in her room, so she used the one in the kitchen to call Mr. Harper's office line. His secretary answered and sounded skeptical when Marian told her it was an urgent matter. It wasn't just that the secretary was a stuck-up bitch—although she totally was—it was just that there was something about Marian's voice that made it difficult for people to take her seriously.

"I'm telling you right now, Barbara," said Marian, doing her best to keep her volume down. "If you don't put him on the phone right now, you're going to regret it big time."

"Are you drunk or something? Because I can never tell with you."

"I mean it," Marian insisted. "Put Mr. Harper on the phone."

Finally, Barbara put the call through. Marian gave Mr. Harper a rough sketch of the morning's events, starting with the discovery of Shane's body and finishing up with how she'd seen Lady Lillian hand the keys to the beach house to that lady cop.

"The vibe around here is getting really bad, too," she told him. "I don't even need to do a psychic reading to pick up on it."

Mr. Harper seemed to growl on the other end of the line. "Never mind the vibes. What's going on right now?"

"Mr. Abilene and the lady cop are going to the beach house. They left about twenty minutes ago."

"Twenty minutes?" Mr. Harper sounded angry. "And you just thought to call me now?"

"I had to start getting lunch ready all by myself. The police wouldn't allow the kitchen staff onto the property until they're done poking around the servants' quarters. And one more thing, you need to have a talk with your secretary about her manners."

The phone went dead before she could offer further suggestions.

"Well, okay, whatever." Marian shrugged and hung up the phone.

It sure was a bummer about Shane. He could be a real doofus sometimes, but he had some good qualities too, like that thing he learned in France, and he usually smelled nice. She couldn't understand why someone would kill him. But that was okay. She couldn't understand half of what was going on in this house lately, but that didn't bother her too much. She was used to not understanding things. For a long time, this had bothered her, but the older she got, the less she minded. The way the world was going, she figured it was better to not think too hard about anything.

Cody drove the Datsun to the beach house with Bev riding shotgun. On the way, they discussed the case. Bev told him that Arledge had Stewart pegged as the prime suspect in Shane's murder. A revenge killing was his theory. Cody tried not to laugh at that one.

"What, you don't think Stewart is capable of something like that?" she asked. "Trust me, the lieutenant has seen plenty in his time."

"I agree that Arledge is a hell of an investigator," Cody said as he brought the Datsun to a stop outside the Chamberlain beach house. "But he's missing the obvious."

"You mean how Stewart is so gay he might as well be wearing a neon sign that says so," Bev said. "Still, jealousy is a weird thing, and gay or not, Anita is still his wife, and that's more than enough for motive."

"Yeah, I guess. He certainly had the opportunity too, but I

still don't buy Stewart as a killer. It's too simple." Cody put the car in Park and got out.

"Hey, there's nothing wrong with simple."

"Not a damn thing," Cody agreed. "But how many times does solving a case like this turn out to be simple?"

Bev didn't have an answer for that one.

They used the key Lady Lillian had given them to get into the beach house. Like the Chamberlain estate, the place was well-appointed. It looked like a photo spread from a home decorating magazine. They headed straight for the bedroom. Cody recognized the bed from the photos Arledge had shown Lady Lillian.

"Wow," Bev said. "No wonder Shane and Anita used this place for a love nest. Pretty swanky, don't you think?"

"It's not too shabby."

"What do you hope to find here?" Bev asked. "The place looks spotless."

"Oh, you know, clues, photos, electronics…" Cody shrugged. "You're familiar with how I operate. I like to cover all the angles."

"Yeah… I know all about your coverage."

Cody smiled and let instinct take the wheel. The investigation could wait. After all, it wasn't like Shane was going to get any deader. And besides, Bev had been putting out the signal strong as a south of the border radio station for quite a while. She looked at him the way a half-starved lion eyed a gazelle. Even if he were so inclined, it would be nearly impossible to fend off her advances. Then, Cody had an idea that was either reckless or brilliant. The line between those two could get pretty damn thin in his experience. The idea involved getting Bev in the sack anyway, so it was awful convenient that she was thinking along those same lines.

"You know, Bev," he said, stepping closer until they were toe-to-toe. "You've been looking awfully good since you've been going to the gym."

"I'm glad you noticed." She leaned in for a kiss. "How'd you like to take a break from this nasty murder stuff and investigate something else?"

"I guess it depends on what you have in mind."

Bev got out of her clothes the same way she hit the weights at the gym: quickly and efficiently, with no wasted movements. Before Cody had gotten his pants off, she was already down to her birthday suit. She put her hands on her hips and stepped back, like she was presenting herself for inspection. *If that was the case*, Cody thought, *she passed with flying colors.*

"You think you can bring this bad girl to justice?" she asked.

"I'll give it my best shot," he said.

Once things took a turn towards hot and heavy, it became clear that his best effort wasn't required. Bev jumped in the driver's seat and took over. Like any good cop, she made it clear from the jump who was in charge. She shoved him toward the bedroom and deposited him on the bed with all the gentleness of a bad cop shoving a suspect into the back of a cruiser. Cody was a bit surprised she didn't try to use the handcuffs on him.

As she rolled him onto his back and climbed on top, Cody felt something hard digging into the small of his back. He worked his hand under his back, careful not to throw off Bev's pleasantly aggressive rhythm. She had her eyes closed, moaning as she ran her hands over her breasts, so she didn't notice that the object Cody pulled from beneath him was a remote control. She certainly didn't notice when started pushing buttons or even when he smiled as he watched a video camera spring from its hiding place behind the dresser.

Bingo!

Cody pushed the button to activate the camera, then tossed the remote control onto the nightstand on his right. He pulled Bev down closer to him and smiled over his shoulder at the camera's shiny lens. Then he got back to the business at hand, letting Bev finish before he himself let go. They collapsed in sweaty tangle, both of them panting like runners who just crossed the finish line.

When he regained his composure, Cody said, "Hey, Bev, how'd you like to see a home movie of us?"

She looked at him with half-lidded eyes and sighed. "Sure thing, cowboy."

"I better warn you, it's not quite the kind of thing you show your mom." He grabbed the remote control from the nightstand and used it to fire up the TV across the room. "Amazing what you can do with technology these days, isn't it?"

"And when did you discover that little gadget?"

"I'd rather not say." He hit the Play button and watched Bev's expression change as the TV screen displayed a bird's eye view of their romp in the sheets. "What do you think? Looks like my kind of soap opera."

"Shane must have been a fan of those candid camera shows." Bev slid out of bed. She snatched the tape from the camera. "I'll keep this, if you don't mind."

"A little souvenir, huh?"

They padded into the living room and put on enough of their discarded clothing to make themselves decent. Cody was just starting to consider asking for a copy of the video when he heard the sound of a car door slamming.

"Bev, you hear that?" he asked.

"Yeah," she replied. "Sounds like we got visitors."

The Richards brothers, Max and Tommy, liked to think of themselves as the sort of smooth assassins they'd seen in James Bond movies, or at the very least, like the bad guys in TV cop shows. But the truth was, they were simply violent Neanderthals whose only marketable skill was roughing people up. They'd done exactly two hits for a drug dealer named Santos Villegas, and although both jobs had been successful, they were far from experts. But they'd bluffed their way into Jonathan Harper's employ, and lo and behold, the guy had sent them on their first big job.

"Don't fuck this up for us, Tommy. I mean it," Max said as he wheeled the black Corvette onto the oyster shell driveway of the Chamberlain beach house. He was the older of the two and the smartest, which wasn't saying much. Both brothers had repeated so many grades that they were legally allowed to purchase alcohol when they were high school sophomores.

"I won't," Tommy promised. "Christ, you're never going to let me forget that thing with hooker in Vegas, are you?"

"No, I'm certainly not. I send you out to find us some entertainment and you come back with a chick who has a dick like a Schlitz tallboy." Max shook his head.

"How many times I gotta say I'm sorry?"

"I figure at least a couple hundred more." Max parked next to a scratched and dented Datsun Z. He checked his hair in the rearview mirror as he said, "All right, here's how we play it. That front door don't look like much, so I'll go right in. You follow my lead."

"Why do I always have to be in the back?"

Max slapped his brother in the back of the head and said, "Because I'm older and smarter

and you got that long hair makes you look like a faggot. Now quit flapping your lips and get back me up. This dude is supposed to be some hotshot private dick, so he's probably packing serious heat, okay?"

Tommy giggled. "Private dick. That's funny."

"See what I mean about that haircut? Look like a fruit long enough, you start acting like one."

When Max saw the hurt look on his little brother's face, he wished he could take back that faggot remark. But he was tired of Tommy's back talk, and besides, his haircut *did* make him look like some MTV pretty boy.

"Fine, I'll back you up," Tommy said, grabbing his shotgun

from the backseat. "But I get to pick where we have dinner this time."

"You got it, bro. Now, please, for the love of God, get your ass in gear."

They climbed out of the car. Max winced as he watched his little brother go.

"Just announce our fucking presence, why don't you," he muttered as he climbed the steps to the front porch.

Before he kicked the door, he checked the knob. Good thing he did too, because the door was unlocked. If Tommy's car door slamming routine hadn't tipped the targets off, then they might still have the element of surprise on their side. He looked over his shoulder and smiled at his little brother.

They opened the door, and when they weren't greeted with a hail of bullets, they tiptoed inside. Max glanced around, impressed by the richness of the front room. The furniture looked brand new, and the TV was so big it took up a good portion of the wall. There was a wet bar in one corner, and the shelf behind it was stocked with an impressive array of high-dollar liquor.

Man, these rich assholes really got it easy, he thought as he crept through the room. *This ain't even their main house, either.*

He paused, shaking himself out of his bitter ruminations. There was the sound of running water coming from one of the rooms in the back of the beach house.

"Hey, bro," he whispered, motioning his brother toward the door. "Sounds like the shower is running. Go check it out."

Tommy smiled, hefting his shotgun.

"Go on," Max said. "I'll cover us outside."

It wasn't often that he let Tommy take point on anything this heavy, but he felt guilty about calling him queer and figured what the hell, it couldn't hurt. Even someone as slow and accident prone as Tommy could handle a guy who was bare-ass naked in the shower. He headed for the door, leaving his brother to it.

Tommy had to admit it: he was excited. On all their jobs so far, he'd been strictly backup. Max did the heavy lifting. Hell, Tommy had only pulled the trigger once, and that was after Max had already put two in the dude's back. That had been more of a consolation prize than anything. Now, he was finally getting a chance to show his big brother what he could do.

He took a deep breath and tiptoed into the master bedroom. Like the room at the front of the house, the place was swanky. There was another large screen TV and a king size bed that looked like it had seen recent action. Tommy smiled. Sure, he might have to see some guy's bare ass when he shot him, but maybe there was some broad in the shower with him. Maybe he'd get to see some tits in the bargain. Of course, he'd also have to plug the bitch, and that would be a shame if she was a looker. But that was the way the game was played.

He crept around the bed, heading for the bathroom door. The hinges didn't even make a noise when he pushed the door open and stepped into the steamy bathroom. The shower curtain was translucent plastic, and he could see a pair of figures silhouetted against the wet surface. He reached out, eager to see the shock on their faces when he ripped the curtain back.

*Shit, this is just like that **Psycho** movie*, he thought.

But when he jerked the curtain aside, it was Tommy who was shocked. Yeah, there was a broad in there with the private detective, and yeah, she was a looker. But neither of them was naked. The detective was wearing a pair of black skivvies and the broad was wearing a white undershirt and a pair of thong panties. But that wasn't what caused Tommy's mouth to gape. No, his shock was entirely due to the size of the gun in the man's hand and the fact that it was pointed squarely at Tommy's chest.

"Go for it, punk," the man snarled. "Make my day."

The asshole squeezed off a shot as soon as the words were out of his mouth. But even at a range of a couple feet, his shot went wide of the mark and shattered the mirror behind Tommy's head. Shards of glass blasted against his back. Trembling with relief, he raising the shotgun. Sure, he was shaking so bad from the adrenaline that his aim would probably be just as bad as the detective's. But Tommy had a shotgun, and in a space as small as this bathroom, it was damn near impossible to miss.

"Fuck you!" he screamed.

Tommy's mistake was underestimating the woman. To his misfortune, it was his last mistake. She raised her hand, which held a snub-nose revolver, a real cop type gun. She snapped off two quick shots—*BLAM, BLAM*—that caught Tommy square in the chest, driving him back against the wall. The shotgun fell from his hands.

"Are you serious?" the woman asked incredulously. *"Go for it? Make my day?* Give me a break."

The private dick answered with a shrug.

Tommy slid down the wall and sat down heavily on the damp tile floor. As his consciousness ebbed away, he watched the man and woman step out of the shower. He glanced up at the woman as she stepped over him. Her t-shirt was soaked and it clung to her tits like it was pasted on. She had a nice set on her, all right. Firm and perky with a nipples so hard it was a wonder they hadn't ripped right through the fabric.

Tommy coughed up a mouthful of blood. At least his last sight would be a nice set of tits.

⌖

Cody didn't much care for Bev's sassy remarks, but he let it slide. There was more pressing business than his wounded pride.

He put a hand on her shoulder as they stepped out over the body of the dying thug.

"Careful, Bev. There's probably another one. These assholes always travel in pairs."

And sure enough, as they emerged into the front room, they caught sight of the second thug standing in the doorway at the back of the house. He hesitated just long enough to see their guns, then turned tail and ran.

"This one's mine," Cody said, dashing after him.

He pressed himself against the trunk of a palm tree for cover, took aim, and blasted away. His hot went wide of the mark, hitting one of the potted plants hanging from a trellis in the back-yard. Shards of ceramic and clods of dirt exploded through the air.

"Cody, come on," Bev said from behind him. She side-stepped him and got into her firing stance.

"Look out!" Cody yelled, shielding her with his body. He fired again, and this time succeeded in wounding one of the towering palm trees at the edge of the yard, where patchy scrub grass gave way to white sand.

"Oh, that's too much," Bev said, shouldering past Cody.

She advanced on the thug with her gun raised. Before he could take aim with his shotgun, Bev had put two rounds into his chest. Center mass, bull's-eye. Cody's shooting instructor would have been proud.

"Hey, what are you doing?" Cody asked. "I could've hit him."

Bev rolled her eyes. "Really?"

"Okay, okay," Cody sighed. He raised his hands and struck a karate pose. "It's these hands that are lethal weapons. They're all I need."

"Sure thing, tough guy. Just be careful when you play with yourself." She turned and headed back into the house.

After they got dressed, Cody fixed a couple of drinks. Bev may have been a tough cop with deadly aim, but Cody could tell she still needed something to take the edge off after sending two idiots to their final reward.

"Here you go," he said, passing her a gin and tonic, then taking a seat next to her on the couch.

"Let me ask you something," she said. "Did you just jump in bed with me because you wanted to see how Shane's video setup worked?"

"You know me better than that. Frankly, I'm shocked you'd even suggest such a thing."

"Right." She rolled her eyes and took a sip of her drink and asked, "So who knew we were coming out here?"

"I almost hate to say," he sighed.

"Lady Lillian?" She took a second, bigger sip of her drink.

"You got it."

"Damn it. I mean…" She trailed off for a second, glancing toward the master bedroom. "Well, I have to call this in. I'll tell the Lieutenant what happened here. It was a good shoot, no question. But it would be better if you made yourself scarce. Otherwise, you'll end up down at the station, answering questions for hours."

"Okay, babe. I hate leaving you here on your own, but I guess you're right." Cody nodded. "If you're sure you can handle this mess, I need to head to my boat and pick up a few things. Call my service if you need me."

She asked for one last kiss before he left. He was happy to oblige.

Chapter Ten

Cody left the beach house feeling guilty. The situation was nothing Bev couldn't handle. She was a decorated officer of the law, after all, and it was a clear cut case of self-defense. Still, he couldn't help feeling like she wouldn't have been involved in this mess if not for him requesting her presence at the crime scene.

He slid into the driver's seat and gunned the Datsun's engine. Ramona's modifications were top notch. The engine sounded like a hungry beast when Cody revved it up. But despite that heavy-duty engine, it was still just a Datsun, and each one of those throaty roars felt like they might shake the puny exterior to pieces.

Cody put it in gear and headed down the long driveway. He glanced in the rearview mirror and told his reflection, "Come on, man. Bev can handle this. Hell, she didn't even need your help plugging those two sons of bitches."

On the way back to the marina, Cody tuned the radio to the local rock station and did his best to puzzle out the situation. He just couldn't believe that Lady Lillian would have sent a couple of gun thugs to the beach house. After all, she was the one who hired him to look into her family in the first place. It didn't make sense to suspect her. But then, if she wasn't the one who sent a couple killers after him, who was?

This calls for some brain food, he thought.

He wheeled the Datsun into the parking lot of the first convenience store he came across. When in doubt, Cody always went for his favorite snack: a peanut brittle candy bar with a cold R.C. Cola to wash it down. His cousin Rowdy swore by the Moon Pie/R.C. combo, but Cody preferred a little crunch in his snacks. Bev would have given him no end of shit for "treating his body like a garbage can," as she so eloquently put it, but she considered a salad to be a meal, whereas Cody thought of it as a prelude to a nice medium rare T-bone.

He was smiling to himself and unwrapping his candy bar as he crossed the parking lot when he heard a sadly familiar voice calling out to him.

"Hey, boy, let's go! Let's get it on one more time! *Yeehaw!* Let's race!"

Cody knew without looking that the voice belonged to P.L. Buffington. The backing chorus of hoots and hollers was none other than Doreen and Bobo.

"Come on, guys," Cody pleaded. "I really don't have time for this…"

"Hear that, Daddy?" Bobo guffawed. "Ol' Cody is yellow! I beat him one time and all the sudden, he's a weak sister!"

"Look, Bobo, the last person I'm afraid of is you," said Cody through a mouthful of candy bar. "But all I got at the moment is this little Datsun. It wouldn't be fair going against that souped-up Caddy you got there."

He had all the faith in the world in Ramona's modifications, but Bobo was leaning against the hood of an El Dorado that was certainly amped up to ridiculous levels. Bobo might not have cared if a single meaningless race put his ride out of commission, but the Datsun was the only set of wheels Cody currently had. Losing his ride would put a serious cramp in his investigation.

"Well, now," P.L. said, slinging his arm around Doreen's considerable shoulders. "I guess that old Abilene grit must have skipped a generation."

Every man had his soft spot, and Cody supposed he was no different. His family's reputation on the racetrack was the one thing that could spur him to such a stupid decision.

"All right, you pack of squirrel-eating lunatics," he said, slapping the Datsun's hood. "I'll see you out at Dry Creek."

The Dry Creek Race Complex was an abandoned racetrack outside of town. Once a popular spot on the west coast circuit, it had been supplanted by newer, more conveniently located race tracks like the one at Willow Springs. Now, it was a dusty two mile circle of buckling asphalt surrounding by rusting bleachers that looked like they might collapse under the slightest pressure. It was a popular spot with amateur dragsters, but Cody thought it should be condemned. Still, it was the closest spot for a race, and if he was going to pursue this stupidity, he figured he might as well get it over with as quickly as possible.

Fifteen minutes after Bobo laid down the challenge, they were side-by-side at the starting line, revving their engines. Standing in the breakdown lane with Doreen at his side, P.L. produced a pistol from the inside pocket of his seersucker sport coat and fired it in the air.

Cody put the hammer down, and the Datsun's engine responded. The hood vibrated so hard Cody was afraid that high-tuned engine might jump right out of the car. Still, he managed to keep pace with Bobo's Caddy until the second turn. Cody downshifted—a classic mistake with a car that small— and felt the clutch slip. He recovered in less than a couple seconds, but that was all the time Bobo needed to take the lead.

"Well, shit," Cody said as he crossed the finish line in second place.

Bobo bailed out of his car as soon as it came to a stop. He trotted onto the track in front of Cody and turned his back. P.L. and Doreen were soon at his side, laughing like lunatics as they turned their backs to Cody.

Just what the hell are they up to? he wondered.

The Buffingtons didn't keep him in suspense very long. With such synchronized precision that Cody knew they'd practiced for hours, the family exposed their backsides. P.L. dropped his pants, Bobo popped the tabs on his overalls and let them fall, and Doreen hiked up her skirt. P.L. had the word "WE" stitched on the seat of his jockey shorts. Doreen, standing between her husband and her son, exposed a pair of bright red panties emblazoned with the word "ARE." Finally, Bobo displayed a pair of polka dot boxers with "#1" written on the back.

"You see that?" P.L. shouted over his shoulder. "The Buffingtons is number one!"

Cody just sat there and took the abuse. What else could he do? It was the second time in a row that moron Bobo had beaten him. He vowed that the next race would have a different outcome.

It damn well better, he thought. *If I don't whip their ass, my daddy is gonna whip mine.*

With all the time he'd wasted with the Buffingtons, it was night before Cody made it back to the marina. Something was wrong under the Datsun's hood. Ever since the race, it had been slipping gears like crazy. Cody hoped Ramona wouldn't take it too hard when he told her. Of course, he would be more than happy to console her if it came to that.

The hinges squealed as Cody opened the caboose-motif door. He made a mental note to squirt some WD-40 on them next chance he got, then stepped aboard the *Malibu Express*. He'd only been gone a couple days, but it felt like forever since he'd been home. A few hours' sleep in his own bed was just what the doctor ordered. Then, maybe he could untangle the web of intrigue spreading out from the Chamberlain estate.

He climbed onto the deck and dug his keys out of his pocket. He'd just stuck his key in the lock on the cabin door when a faint noise caught his ear. No mistaking it, that sound was the hinges of the caboose door protesting as someone opened them.

Here we go again, he thought.

A quick sideways glance confirmed his suspicions. Three shadowy figures were doing their best to sneak down the slip. One the figures stationed himself just inside the door while the other two continued their slow approach.

Well, if it ain't my friends, the Apostles. They were about as subtle as a sledgehammer in their approach. Guys that big aren't built for stealth.

Cody stepped inside the cabin and drew his gun. He looked around for the best place to set up his counter-attack. But then he heard the unmistakable sound of women's laughter coming from behind him. He turned and found himself looking down at his two newest neighbors. They were bikini-clad as usual and seated on his couch, each of them holding a wine cooler. It looked like Faye and May had planned a little ambush of their own, and at the worst possible time.

"We were hoping you'd show up soon," Faye said. She pushed her chest forward in a pose that would, under normal circumstances, have gotten Cody's engine firing on all cylinders.

"Yeah, we've missed you," May added, striking a similar pose.

Doing his best to keep any panic from creeping into his voice, he asked them to follow him to the bedroom. They tittered with excitement and did as he asked. Once they were inside, he sat them down on the bed.

"All right, Mr. Detective," Faye said in a voice slurred by copious amounts of Bartles and Jaymes. "Let's get it on."

"Yeah," May agreed. "Finally we get some attention around here."

Cody shushed them. "Now, look here, girls. Don't ask me any questions, okay? As soon as I tell you, hit the floor, cover your heads, and don't move until the coast is clear. You got that?"

"Oh, this is kinky," Faye chirped.

"Yeah," May agreed. "I love kinky stuff. This is gonna be fun."

Cody shushed them again, then got into his best imitation of Bev's firing stance. He kept his gun trained on the door as Faye and May did their best to stifle their laughter. Judging by the number of empty wine cooler bottles he'd seen in the living area, their restraint was admirable.

There was a series of muted footfalls just outside the bedroom door. Cody tensed, bracing himself for what lay ahead. The footsteps stopped. The sound of labored breathing took their place. At least Cody knew which one of the Apostles was coming for him first. It had to be Matthew. No way his gym rat partners got winded just walking onto a boat.

The heavy breathing paused so Matthew could grunt his version of a war cry, then the door burst open.

"Now!" Cody yelled.

For once, Faye and May actually did as they were told without protest. Screaming, they hit the floor just as Matthew turned sideways to wedge himself through the door. Cody took aim and fired. He'd been trying to blow Matthew's brains out of his thick skull, but as usual, his aim left plenty to be desired. Instead of punching a hole through Matthew's head, the bullet only winged him, clipping off the top half of his ear.

Matthew's war cry changed to a yelp of surprised pain. He clapped one hand to his wounded ear. Blood squelched between his fingers. Had Cody not known better, he might have thought he'd dealt the fat man a near-deadly blow. But hid childhood wrestling bouts with Rowdy had taught him that even a small wound to any part of the head could be a real gusher.

Cody fired again, this time missing the target entirely. The bullet took out a decent sized chunk of the doorframe instead. Splinters rained down on Matthew's head. He attempted to bring the shotgun around, maybe to attempt a one-handed shot, but the long barrel caught on the door and the gun thumped on the floor. He turned and ran for the exit.

"Girls, I need you to stay right here, understand?" Cody said in the sternest voice he could manage. "Do not leave this room under any circumstances."

Faye and May had sobered up considerably in the last few seconds. Amazingly, they didn't appear the least bit horny anymore. It was like Cody was seeing them for the first time. They clung to one another, nodding furiously as they cowered on the floor beside the bed.

Cody charged off in pursuit of the wounded Apostle. But now that Matthew was out of the confined space of the boat, he was stepping lightly. Well, as lightly as a man of his size could manage anyway. He had a considerable lead on Cody and was nearly through the caboose door before Cody could even get a decent shot off. He took careful aim, but didn't fire. It was too dark to know for sure that no innocent bystanders were lurking behind nearby.

"Come on, boys!" Matthew shouted, his feet pounding down the boat slip. "He just shot my ear off!"

His gym rat buddies—Luke and Mark—half-turned in Cody's direction. Even at this distance, he knew they were running the odds in their steroid-addled brains. They were trying to decide if they could close the distance between themselves and Cody before he could get off two shots. Had they known about Cody's accuracy-challenged marksmanship, they might have decided to risk it. But for all they knew, he was a crack shot, so they turned and followed Matthew up to the parking lot, where they piled into a car. Tires squealing, the car sped away without its headlights on. In a moment, they were gone, swallowed up by the night.

"Damn," Cody muttered. "Guess I'll have to settle for getting you next time."

He lowered his gun and went back inside to comfort the girls. Unfortunately, this wasn't going to be the kind of physical contact they'd been expecting when they sneaked onto his boat.

Chapter Eleven

The ringing phone jolted Cody awake. He'd fallen asleep sitting up on the couch, hat tipped over his eyes and gun in hand. He jumped so suddenly that it was a miracle he didn't wind up shooting himself in the foot. Once he'd managed to take a couple deep breaths, he dropped the gun on the end table and snatched the receiver off its cradle.

"Hello?" he groaned, scrubbing his sleep-filmed eyes with the back of his hand.

"Cody, it's Bev."

"Jesus, Bev, it's…" He glanced at his watch, but his eyes were too bleary to read it. "Well, I don't know what time it is, but it feels like the crack of dawn."

"Sorry, but this couldn't wait." She sounded tired. Maybe dealing with the fallout of the shooting at the beach house had taken a lot out of her. "The Lieutenant decided to arrest Stewart Chamberlain for Shane's murder. He found some photos of Shane and Stewart together. I guess I don't have to tell you what I mean by *together*. I'm at the Chamberlain estate right now, and the whole house is in an uproar."

"Listen, Bev, I got some news for you too." He stood up, stretching the phone cord to its limit so he could duck into the galley and get some coffee started. "Try to remember how highly you think of me and try not to get too angry. Before you got to the scene, I found another roll of film in Shane's drawer."

"You held that out on me?" She sounded more disappointed than angry.

"Well, look, it was my case first, wasn't it?" He hit the button on the coffee pot and edged back into the front room, where he collapsed on the couch.

"It's not your case anymore, cowboy. We're beyond the bounds of private investigation," she said. "I sure would like to get that film developed, though. It could be the thing that blows this case wide open."

"Whatever's on it must be important. Some of Jonathan Harper's goons tried to kill me for it last night. Not to mention that little scene at the beach house yesterday."

The front door swung open and Cody's neighbors slipped in uninvited, as usual. May was carrying a cheerleader's baton, which she flourished as she entered. She parked her butt on the couch right next to him while Faye ducked into the galley and poured him a cup of coffee. When she returned, she'd shed her bikini top. She presented him with the steaming mug then sat down on the other side of him. As hard as he tried, Cody just couldn't be mad at Faye and May. They were too damn cute for that. They tittered and giggled, snugged up against him thigh-to-thigh like a couple of sexy bookends.

"Cody, it sounds like someone's there," Bev said. "Do you have company? Is something going on?"

"Well, nothing out of the usual." And because honesty was always the best policy, he added, "Just a topless lady serving me my morning coffee while her sexy friend twirls a baton." Then, in a reversal of that best policy, "Get serious, Bev. Of course I'm alone. You're just hearing the TV."

"Sorry, I guess I'm still a little frazzled."

May dropped her baton and tugged off her top. With her on

one side and Faye on the other, Cody hardly knew where to look.

"Yeah, me too…" He paused to clear his throat as the ladies ran their hands over their breasts, giving him a good show as they perked up their nipples. "Knowing Shane, whatever's on that film isn't something we can just drop off at the corner drugstore. And I'm not ready to hand it over to the cops. No offense, but I'd like to see this thing through. Listen, I might have a solution to that problem. Let me call you back in a few."

He hung up before she had a chance to protest. It wasn't easy to dial a phone with two glorious sets of melons staring him in the face, but Cody overcame that adversity, pleasant as it was. He dialed his answering service. Sally answered in her usual breathy purr.

"Sally's Lip Service, may I help you?"

"Hey, Sally, it's Cody Abilene. Can you get me June Khnockers at Willow Springs?"

"Oh, Cody, baby. You sound flustered. Where are you?" she asked.

"Nowhere special," he answered. "Just hanging out on my boat."

"Baby, I'd love to raise your sail. Maybe tighten your jib sheet. You can batten down my hatch. I just can't wait to do it port and starboard, fore and aft."

Cody groaned inwardly. "Sally, all that sounds great, but I've got all I can handle this morning."

"Sure thing, baby. Now, that's Khnockers with an 'h,' right? Tell me honestly, does she give better lip service than I do?"

"That's a negatory on that one, Sally." Truthfully, Cody would be hard-pressed to rate one of them over the other. They were both dynamite in the sack.

"Then I'll be happy to get her for you," Sally said.

While he held the line, Cody fended off his neighbors to ask how they managed to slip past his security system yet again. He also reminded them that the *Malibu Express* was a bit of a dangerous place these days. They didn't miss a beat. It was like they'd forgotten about the prior night's events.

"Cody, you know you like having us around," May insisted.

"Body by Fisher, brains by Mattel," Cody sighed.

If the ladies caught the reference, they certainly didn't show it. They went right on with their private peep show, slipping off the bottoms of their bathing suits to let him get a look at the entire package.

Finally, June got on the line. "Hey, Cody, you coming by the track today? Mario tweaked the Chevy's engine so I'm going to take it for a spin."

"I'd love to, but I also gotta ask you for a bit of a favor. I have this roll of film I need developed. You happen to know if Rodney will be around?"

"Yeah, actually she should be here any minute. She wants to take some photos of me for the next issue of *Auto Club*."

"Great," Cody said, trying to keep his voice even as Faye hit her knees and started trying to lower the zipper on his pants. "I'll be by there in a couple hours."

"Great, I'll see you then," June replied. She smooched the phone before she hung up.

Cody's zipper was stubborn, but Faye was persistent. He had no doubt he'd be swinging in the wind in no time. Still, he managed to dial the number for the Chamberlain estate and get Bev on the line.

"Bev, I think I got a solution to our problem," he said as soon as she answered. "Can you wait for me there at the Chamberlain estate? I'll pick you up as soon as I can. We have to go out to the Willow Springs Raceway."

"That's perfect. I need to console Lady Chamberlain about her son's arrest. When can I expect you?"

"Well, I got a couple things I need to take care of over here, but I'll get out there as soon as I can." He dropped the phone back on the cradle just as Faye succeeded in getting his zipper to work. He stood up so she could finish the job without catching the zipper's teeth on any sensitive parts.

"I thought I was going to have to do all the work," Faye laughed as she tugged his pants down.

Cody opened his mouth to answer, but before he could get a single word out, May planted her lips on his. Cody knew he didn't have time for fooling around, but these ladies were a force of nature. And sometimes you just gotta relax and let nature take its course.

⚓

At the Chamberlain estate, the entire household was indeed in an uproar. Well, almost all of it, anyway. Marian wasn't shocked in the least to hear that the police had arrested Stewart. She knew all about the photos of him and Shane sharing some naughty time. It seemed to her that Shane had learned plenty of tricks during his time in France. Some of the stuff in those photos was positively exotic.

Marian stayed out of the way and kept her eyes and ears open. She'd been instructed to monitor the phone calls made by the lady cop. It was easy work. Much easier than clearing dishes or gathering dirty laundry. All she had to do was listen carefully on the extension in the kitchen and write down anything that might be of interest.

That last phone call between the lady cop and the cowboy private detective had been most informative. Although there really wasn't any need for her to write down the information, Marian did it anyway. It was better that people thought she was stupid. That way, they never expected her to be mixed up in anything too complicated. And this stuff was pretty darn complicated. Even though she wasn't as stupid as people assumed, she didn't quite understand everything that was going on. She was also certain that she didn't really want to understand it. Anything that involved people as rich and powerful as the Chamberlain family and Jonathan Harper was way out of her league.

As soon as Marian hung up the phone, the lady of the house had begun ringing a bell to summon her. There was a time when Marian could have happily jammed that bell down Lady Lillian's throat and not felt one twinge of guilt. Now, she just didn't care anymore. As soon as she collected her pay, she was hitting the road. It was time for a change of scenery.

She wrote the words "Willow Springs Raceway" in big, loopy script and the notepad, then tore off the sheet. Humming to herself, she walked to the library, where Lady Lillian had been stationed all morning.

"Well, darling, don't keep me in suspense," Lady Lillian said. "Wherever are those two going?"

Smiling like a dutiful maid who was happy to be of service, Marian handed over the sheet of paper.

"Willow Springs Raceway, eh?" Lady Lillian looked thoughtful as she crumbled the paper into a tight little ball. "That will be all, Marian. You may have the rest of the day off."

"Thank you, thank you so much," she gushed. She turned around and got the hell out of there before the old bat could change her mind.

She hurried to her third floor bedroom. Once inside, she locked the door behind her and stripped off her maid's uniform. All in all, working at the Chamberlain estate wasn't a bad job— she'd certainly done worse—but she hated the uniform. She'd worn a similar uniform for a prior job, but that was a movie gig and it only required her to wear the maid uniform for a few minutes at the beginning of the scene. That had been a real bummer. She'd put a lot of effort into memorizing her lines and then found out that most guys just fast forward until the clothes come off. Needless to say, her scene in *Naughty French Maids vol. 17* didn't catapult her to a successful film career. So she'd put in for a job at the Chamberlain estate. Pretty disappointing to have to wear the same uniform again.

Once she'd gotten down to her bra and panties, she made a phone call to her other boss. She told Mr. Harper the same thing she'd told Lady Lillian, only she wasn't expected to pass him a little sheet of paper.

"Thank you," Mr. Harper said. "Marian, I'm having a party on Sunday evening. Some very important investors will be there. I was wondering if you could, ah, provide some companionship for some of the men. Perhaps wear that uniform?"

"Ugh, not interested. I'm getting the hell out of this place. You can wire my money to my account, but I'm not doing any more parties. I'm going to lay on a beach for a while."

"Suit yourself," he replied. "But these investors can get pretty loose with their cash once the champagne starts flowing. If you reconsider, give me a call."

"Whatever." She hung up the phone and dragged her suitcase out of her closet.

⛴

Cody made two stops on the way to the Chamberlain estate. The first was at a convenience store to grab a peanut brittle bar and an RC. After a morning between Faye and May, he needed to replenish some calories. The second was at Mitch Harris' garage to pick up his daddy's Olds.

Cody pulled the Datsun into the lot just as Mitch was running a rag over the Olds' glossy red paint job.

"Wow, buddy, I'm impressed," Cody said as he climbed out of the Datsun. "She looks like she just came off the assembly line. Hell, she looks better than that."

"Shit, it wasn't nothing..." Mitch shrugged. "And I figure it's the least I can do after what your daddy did for me back in Tampa."

Jimmy Dean Abilene had helped pull Mitch out of a burning car at a regional qualifier race ten years ago. It had cost Cody's father the win, but it had saved Mitch from a fiery death. It was a story that had a happy ending all around. Jimmy Dean had taken first in his next three races, which more than made up for the loss in Tampa, and Mitch had taken it as a sign to get out of the racing business and return to his first love: modifying engines.

"Hell, he was happy to do it," Cody said, grabbing his wallet from his back pocket. "Now how much do I owe you?"

Mitch waved off the offer. "You know better than that, man. Abilene money will never be good here as long as I'm drawing breath."

Cody knew better than to argue. He tucked his wallet away.

"Just wait until you get a taste of what this baby can do." Mitch's face beamed as he handed over the keys. "Had to chain the engine down just to keep her from jumping right through the hood. And that special system under the hatchback should blow by that redneck family."

Cody sighed and shook his head. "Those damn Buffingtons..."

"Speaking of which," Mitch continued, "I ought to have your DeLorean ready to go in a few days. There wasn't anything wrong with it, so I suspect your nemesis was using nitrous or some such to get an advantage. But I did some tinkering and I think I got your car in the best shapes she's ever been in. I'm just waiting on a part to come in and she'll be greased lightning."

"I sure do appreciate it, Mitch. You mind if I leave this Datsun here for a day or two?

There's a certain lady who might appreciate having it back. But I'm in a bit of hurry, so I can't get it back to her right now."

"Hell, that's no problem. I can do you one better. You give me an address, I can have a couple of my guys drop it off for you."

Cody shook his head. "Thanks for the offer, but it's a delivery I'd rather make in person. But I'm under the gun with work right now."

"Understood."

Under normal circumstances, Cody would have loved nothing more than to hang around Mitch's garage all day, talking about engines while they worked their way through a 12-pack of Miller High Life. But the investigation was heating up so fast it might just burst into flames if Cody didn't stay on top of it.

He thanked Mitch one more time and climbed into the car. The engine thrummed like the world's biggest tiger purring contentedly after a vicious kill.

"Just one gentle reminder," Mitch said, leaning into the open driver's side window. "That monster you got sitting in the hatchback? Ain't a state in the union where that shit is street legal. You get caught, you tell them you never heard the name Mitch Harris."

"I read you loud and clear, buddy." Cody tipped him a salute as he drove off the lot.

Bev was waiting at the front gate of the Chamberlain estate. She was pacing back and forth in front of the guard shack, looking like she'd had one too many cups of coffee. Cody could damn near feel the nervous energy coming off her as she climbed into the passenger seat.

"What the hell took you so long?" she asked.

"I told you I had a couple things to take care of." He gunned the engine, burning rubber down the short access road. He pulled onto the highway without even tapping the brakes.

"Oh, sure." Bev shook her head and gave him a look that said she wasn't buying it. "And did these two things have big tits and cute names like Bambi and Trixie?"

That was the thing about getting intimate with a skilled detective. They always had you dead to rights. Cody knew better than to take the bait.

"What do you think of my daddy's Olds?" he asked. "You know, he's a guy who loves gadgets and you wouldn't believe what's sitting under that hatchback..."

"Wait a second," Bev interrupted. "I think you got a tail. Left lane, two cars back. Dark brown Cadillac. Been on you ever since we came down the on-ramp."

Cody glanced at the rearview. That brown Caddy was pulling ahead, overtaking the car on its left. It slid into the lane right behind him.

"They get any closer, they'll drive right up my butt," Cody said. "No doubt about them tailing us. I recognize that car. The boys riding in it paid me a visit at the marina last night. It wasn't exactly a social call. I'm going to give them the shake. If you're not buckled up already, better do it now."

If nothing else, it gave Cody the chance to open up the Olds and see what she could do. He didn't need to engage any of those super-secret modifications. This was far too easy to require drastic measures.

One mile before their exit, Cody whipped the Olds into the left lane and stomped on the accelerator. He pulled ahead of an 18-wheeler. In the side mirror, he watched the Cadillac slide into the left lane, but the car ahead of them prevented them from passing as quickly as they would have liked. By the time they'd pulled in front of the big rig, Cody had already exited.

"Nice driving, cowboy," Bev said. "You sure know how to slip into tight spaces."

Getting off the highway should have added a few minutes to the trip, but Cody knew every back road in the county. He had them at the Willow Springs Raceway right on schedule. June waved to him as he wheeled the Olds into the parking lot. She was sitting on the hood of her car, decked out in her full racing gear.

"Hey, Cody!" she called, sliding off the car and skipping over to meet him. Her smile faltered just a bit when she saw Bev climbing out of the passenger side door. She looked over at

Cody, raising her eyebrows and asking, "Oh, I didn't know you were bringing someone along for the ride. Who is she, anyway, your older sister?"

The last thing Cody needed was for these two to start up a cat fight. Although the idea struck him as entertaining in theory, there just wasn't have time for it. They'd given the bozos in the Caddy the slip for now, but who knew if they'd be back. Thankfully, Bev didn't take the bait. She just smiled right back at June.

"June, I'd like you to meet my friend Beverly McAfee," Cody said. "Detective Sergeant Beverly McAfee, I mean. She's helping me on a case. Is Rodney around?"

June nodded in the direction of the announcer's tower. "Yeah, she's up top. She's expecting you."

"Thanks."

Cody got the hell out of there before the women could start doing more than just giving each other the stink eye.

"Just helping you out on a case, huh?" Bev laughed as they climbed the stairs to the announcer's booth.

"Come on, Bev. Cut me some slack, huh? I'm only human, after all."

"Don't sweat it, cowboy. I gave up tying you down a long time ago."

Rodney was waiting for them outside the door. Cody introduced the two women to one another and sighed with relief that it went much smoother this time. He dug the roll of film out of his pocket and passed to Rodney, asking her if she could develop it.

"It doesn't have to be good," he said. "Just fast."

"Fast but not good, huh?" Rodney smiled. "Sounds like most men I know. But I bet you'd be different, Cody."

"So, that's a yes to my question about getting those developed?" Cody asked, eager to steer the conversation to a subject that wouldn't provoke Bev's wrath.

"Sure," Rodney answered. "There's a little darkroom in here for when races have a photo finish. It's not as good as my home studio, though. You should come see it sometime, Cody. I think you might find it interesting. I could explain all the ins and outs, show you how I handle the equipment."

"I'm sure he'd love to check you out," Bev said. "Check out your darkroom, I mean."

Rodney didn't seem bothered by the remark. She said, "It's pretty close quarters in there. How about you guys wait out here and I'll call you when it's done?"

"Sounds great to me," Cody replied.

He and Bev rested their elbows on the railing and watched June do laps in her Chevy until Rodney hollered for them to come inside and have a look. They went inside and walked through the cramped and cluttered announcer's area to the dark room on the backside of the tower. Rodney ushered them into the red-lit space. A couple newly developed photos hung like clean laundry on a clothesline. Rodney squeezed on of the clothespins and pass Cody one of the damp 8x10s.

Cody examined the photo. It was a cock-eyed view of someone standing in a doorway.

Although the photo was surprisingly clear, the face was too small to recognize. Still, it was exactly what Cody had hoped it would be: Shane's snapshot of his killer.

"I bet this was what those goons were after last night," he said, passing the photo over to Bev. "I can't quite make out the face. How about you?"

Bev shook her head.

Cody turned to Rodney and asked, "Any chance you can get us an enlargement of the portion with the face?"

"Sure, no sweat." Rodney nodded. "I don't know what camera the photographer was using, but whatever it was, they spent plenty of dough on it. The resolution is good enough that I bet I can blow it up big enough for you to see the face. Might take me a few minutes, but I can do it."

"Thanks a million," Cody said.

He and Bev stepped outside and watched June continue her

daily practice routine. The Chevy's finely tuned engine roared as she hugged the curves.

"She sure can drive, can't she?" Cody said.

"Yeah, and I be that's not all she can do. Or did I misread the situation?" Bev asked.

Cody knew better than to lie to a detective of Bev's caliber. He admitted that she had him dead to rights. He raised his hands in a plea for leniency.

Bev just laughed. "Relax, cowboy. I knew the score before I climbed in the sack with you. I just like watching you squirm."

"You're too much, Bev."

"This thing we got going is good enough for me," she continued. "At least for the time being. Otherwise I'd have you in cuffs by now. Then again, maybe you'd enjoy that."

Rodney spared him further embarrassment by stepping onto the balcony to show them the enlargement she'd just finished.

"How's that, detective?" she asked, passing Bev the photo. "Good enough to make an ID?"

"I'll say." Bev passed the photo to Cody.

"Son of a bitch. I never would have thought…" He shook his head. "Come on, Bev. We better get on this one right away."

He handed the photo to Bev whose eyes widened as recognition dawned. She tucked the photo into her oversized purse.

"Thanks for everything, Rodney," Cody said.

"Don't mention it," she replied. "I'm sure you'll be happy to return the favor somehow. I can think of a few ways right of the top of my head."

"Well, how about you make a list and we'll get around to it." Cody grabbed Bev's arm and guided her to the staircase.

Chapter Twelve

Heart attacks ran in Matthew's family. His father, his grandfather, and two uncles had succumbed to massive heart attacks before they were eligible to collect social security. The doctor kept telling Matthew he was headed for the same thing if he didn't cut down on his McDonald's habit and find a way to manage his anger. Easy for him to say. That doctor didn't have to work with a couple of nitwits like Mark and Luke. It was like the steroids had shrunken their brains. Matthew was usually joking when he suggested that, but lately he'd started to wonder. He'd heard that the 'roids could shrink your balls, so he supposed anything was possible.

By the time they'd doubled back to the Willow Springs Raceway, he was ready to blow a gasket. Not only was his bandaged ear throbbing like a son of a bitch, his patience for his partners' stupidity was worn completely away. Once they dealt with this Cody Abilene asshole, he was going to ask Mr. Harper to either get him new partners or move him to another department. Maybe driving the man's limo would be a better gig than doing his dirty work.

"Just park the goddamn car," he growled. "We'll find that red Olds and wait for the asshole to show up."

"Don't know what you're so mad about," Mark said, pouting like a scolded child. "I said I was sorry, didn't I?"

Matthew let that one go. Anything he could say at this point would be a waste of breath. Mark whipped the Caddy into the first available space, and the trio of enforcers bailed out, slamming the doors behind them. Matthew moved to the back of the car and popped the trunk, muttering under his breath about steroids and shrunken brains. Inside the trunk was a large duffel bag filled with weapons. He unzipped it and grabbed two shotguns, which he passed to Mark and Luke.

"Think you boys can manage these without blowing your own balls off?" he asked, staring hard at the two idiots, daring them to question his leadership. When neither of them offered a response, he grabbed his Uzi out of the bag. He hesitated for a moment, glancing at his partners to make sure they weren't watching too closely. Then he grabbed a grenade from the bag. He'd been saving that little guy for a special occasion, and something told him that today might be the day. He stuffed the grenade into the pocket of his windbreaker and slammed the trunk.

It turned out that they didn't have to go looking for Abilene and his cop girlfriend. As soon as Matthew and his partners had armed up, the two targets came strolling out of the announcer's tower, easy as you please.

Luke raised his shotgun and took aim, but Matthew grabbed the barrel before he could get a shot off.

"Wait until they come downstairs," he said. "You start shooting now, they'll just hole up on top of that goddamn tower and hold us off until the cops get here. Wait until they make it to the parking lot, then light 'em up, okay?"

"Yeah, I got it," Luke snapped. "Don't have to be such an asshole all the time."

"Pretty please with sugar on top, don't open fire until they get closer." Matthew gritted his teeth to keep from screaming in frustration. "There, is that better?"

Mark smiled, clearly getting a kick out of the situation.

"You think this shit is funny?" Matthew asked.

"No, boss, I just thought of something."

"First time for everything, I guess." Matthew crouched between two cars and motioned the others to follow his example.

Pretty soon, he heard approaching footsteps. Bellowing like a madman, he came up firing. Mark and Luke popped up like they were part of that Whack-A-Mole game at the arcade. Mark tried to fire his shotgun, but he'd neglected to take the safety off.

"Jesus Christ," Matthew muttered, firing off another burst of rounds.

Abilene had his pistol out, and although it was a real Dirty Harry-style hand cannon, the dumb hick couldn't hit the broadside of a barn. One of Matthew's bullets, on the other hand, found its target, hitting the lady cop in the shoulder and spinning her around like a top. She went down, disappearing behind a car. Abilene must have not been hero material after all. He ducked down behind the car where the lady cop had fallen, but a couple seconds later, he popped back up and took off running in the opposite direction, leaving his girlfriend high and dry.

"Come on," Matthew shouted to the two shotgun-wielding clowns. "He's getting away!"

Thankfully, they managed to follow him without argument.

⚓

Cody panicked when he saw Bev go down. He hit the ground beside her, expecting the worst.

"It's okay," she said, pushing herself to a seated position. She leaned back against the car and looked at her wounded shoulder. "No problem, he just winged me. It's just a scratch.

But you better get out of here before they figure out that I'm not dead."

"I can't just leave you here." Cody winced at the sight of her bloody shoulder.

"I can take care of myself. Remember, I'm the one who can actually shoot what I'm aiming for," she reminded him. She winced as she shrugged off her purse's shoulder strap. "Here, the photos are in my purse. Just make sure you don't lose it. That videotape of us is in there too. I'd hate for that to fall into the wrong hands. Now get moving. I can handle these bozos."

Cody nodded. He knew Bev was right. Not only was she a crack shot, she was a cop in a department known for its toughness. If she said she could handle the situation, she meant it.

"Now get out of here before they ventilate your ass," she told him.

"I love it when you talk dirty." He gave her a peck on the cheek then took off running for the opposite side of the racetrack with Bev's purse in one hand and his gun in the other.

June was halfway through her lap, and if he could make it to her in time, he could jump in her car and get the hell out of there. But there was an awful lot of open ground between those two points. He winced at the sound of each gunshot coming from behind him. Matthew must have been plenty pissed off about his having half his ear blown on, because he was shouting between each burst of bullets from his submachine gun. Most of what he shouted was incoherent, but the parts Cody understood were not nice at all. Matthew was calling him every name in the book and a few he'd probably dreamed up just for this occasion.

A bullet whizzed by Cody's head, so close that he could feel his hair move. If this foot chase went on much longer, his luck was bound to run out. Thankfully, his good fortune was still holding up, because June had noticed all the commotion. She pulled the Chevy into the breakdown lane and came out of the car, waving her hands over her head as she trotted across the track to the inside lane.

"Come on, Cody!" she shouted.

He raised his gun and fired blindly, emptying the chamber in what he hoped was the general direction of the three apostles. By the time he made it to the track, his lungs were on fire and his feet felt like two big blisters. He risked a backwards glance and was relieved to see that Matthew, Mark, and Luke had fallen well behind. Matthew may have been plenty pissed off, and the other two may have been covered in muscles, but none of them were built for speed. June's Chevy, on the other hand, was customized for just that purpose.

"What's going on?" June asked. "Are they shooting at you? And since when do you carry a purse?"

"No time to explain," he panted, grabbing her arm and steering her back towards the car. "Let's get the hell out of here. I'll drive. I've always wanted to get behind the wheel of this thing anyway."

"You can drive my car anytime you want, baby," June said.

They clambered into the car. Cody put it in gear and hit the gas. With all that horsepower under the hood, the Chevy was like a rocket.

"There you go, baby," June moaned. The Chevy wasn't the only thing with an over-cranked engine, it seemed. "Drive faster!"

Matthew thought his head was going to explode as he watched Abilene speed away in the race car. He bent over and grabbed his knees, trying to force some air back into his lungs. Luke and Mark stopped alongside him. They didn't seem winded. How was it that they could be in such good shape and so goddamn slow? All those muscles were useless.

"Should we go back for that cop?" Luke asked.

"No, we don't got time for that," Matthew wheezed. "She must have passed that film off to Abilene. That's why he ran out on her. We don't get that film back, we're cooked. Mr. Harper will have his Russian friends throw us in some goddamn gulag."

"That's the soup the commies eat," Mark said, his thick voice full of confidence.

"What you mean? They going to drown us in soup?" Luke asked. "That's fucking weird, man."

"Jesus Christ, you nitwits! A gulag ain't fucking soup!" Now that Matthew had some of his wind back, he could shout. "It's a prison! Borscht is the soup those commies eat!"

He was just about to turn around and begin the long march back to their car when something caught his eyes. There was a big patch of open land on the south side of the raceway. Out in the middle of it, maybe a couple hundred yards from where they stood, was a large building made of corrugated metal and cinderblocks. There was a sign made of weathered, sun-bleached wood on top of the building. The lettering on the sign had probably once been red, but the desert sun and time had bleached it to a dull pink. It read:

HARRY HAUSS HELICOPTER SERVICE AND TOURS
"See the valley in high style!!!"
Certified Technicians On Site

And wouldn't you know it, there was a helicopter just behind the building.

That dope Abilene probably thinks he made a clean getaway in that souped-up race car, Matthew thought. *But I bet that pretty boy hick never considered that we might have air support.*

"What are you looking at?" Mark asked, raising his arm to scratch his sweaty pit.

"Come on, boys," Matthew said, pointing at the building. "I got an idea."

Once they made it to a straight stretch of road, Cody stomped harder on the accelerator, gripping the wheel so tightly that his knuckles popped. The Chevy's heavily modified engine roared in response. The speedometer climbed past 120 mph and Cody forced himself to look away. Having grown up at auto race-tracks, he knew all too well what would happen if he wiped out at that speed.

June wasn't helping matters one bit. All the fast driving had turned her on, apparently, because she had wiggled out of the top portion of her jumpsuit. She bounced around in the passenger seat, jiggling her tits and laughing like a lunatic.

"Not really the best time for that," Cody said, although he risked a quick peek.

"I see you looking," she squealed. "You know you can't resist me. Come on, unzip your pants and I'll help you relax."

"Maybe later, I don't know. Right now, I gotta..." he trailed off as checked the rearview mirror. There was heli-copter tailing them. It looked like one of Harry Hauss' chop-pers, but it was flying way too low. Harry was an old fart who did scenic tours. He wasn't the type to come in fast and low like that. Cody had a sinking feeling in the pit of his stomach. That feeling worsened when he saw Matthew lean out of the helicopter's door and raise his machine gun to his shoulder. Meanwhile, June was getting more and more aggressive.

"Now, June, goddamn it, I can't do that right now," Cody snapped, swatting her hand away from his crotch.

Matthew's gun rattled, its barrel belching smoke. The bullets pinged off the asphalt in front of the car. Cody twitched the wheel to the right and then back. He sure as hell hoped that made them a harder target to hit.

"Oh, come on. You know speed turns me on." June started to wriggle across the center console. She grabbed her breasts, pressing them together. "Don't you want to have some fun? Sure you do. Let's play around a little."

Another burst of machine gun fire went wide left, raising little puffs of dust as the bullets sprayed the shoulder.

"Come on, baby..." June wiggled her breasts in his face. "Don't you like these anymore?"

"Well, yeah, but..." Cody jerked his head to the side and narrowly avoided being blinded by one perfectly pink erect nipple. "Honey, this just ain't the time for it. Those guys shot Beverly and now they're after us!"

"I don't care about that. I want to have fun!"

Cody groaned, craning his neck to see over the tops of June's endowments. "Jesus! Would you put those things away, woman?"

"That's the first time you've ever said that. Are you feeling okay?"

"I've got this thing doing 150 and they're still right on our ass," he pleaded. "You should keep your head down."

"Oh, you want me to put my head down?" June giggled.

Cody had the Olds cranked as high as he could manage. The needle of the tachymeter was crawling into the red. The engine temperature was doing the same. Something was wrong under the hood, and unfortunately, pulling over and letting the pit crew take a look wasn't an option.

Good Lord, can things get any more complicated? Cody wondered.

As if on cue, his thought was answered by a short burst of gunfire. The helicopter dipped even lower, flying alongside the car. June turned in her seat and flashed her tits at them, giving Harry and his captors a good show.

The other two idiots in the helicopter opened fire. Cody figured it was coming, but he

flinched all the same. Those shotguns weren't accurate in the hands of two imbeciles hanging onto helicopter seats for dear life, but they at least twice as loud as Matthew's Uzi. Loud enough to persuade June to finally take their situation seriously. Her smile disappeared. She dropped back into the passenger seat, covering her breasts with her hands like she'd suddenly developed a sense of modesty.

"Oh my God, they're shooting at us!" she wailed.

"You noticed that, huh?" Despite everything, Cody had to laugh. "What do you think I've been trying to tell you for the last five miles?"

"I'm sorry, it's just…" June tucked her goodies back into her jumpsuit and ran the zipper up. "I thought we left them in the dust back there at the track. How did they manage to get a helicopter?"

"It's one of Harry's."

"No way!" June turned her head to look at the low-flying helicopter. "Harry is a family friend. Sure, he's a little weird, but he'd never try to kill us."

"I doubt he has much of a choice. I'm guessing poor Harry is flying with a gun pointed at him."

There was another burst of gunfire. The helicopter was gaining on them every second. If only Cody could make it to the big curve a few miles ahead without getting shot, he might be able to shake them.

And then, suddenly, the helicopter peeled off, heading for the mountains beyond the curve. Cody wondered what the hell they were up to. Maybe they were low on fuel? He supposed that was wishful thinking.

"Hey, where did they go?" June asked.

Cody shook his head. He was starting to get a bad feeling about what lay ahead.

Matthew was getting closer and closer to losing his goddamn mind. The old son of a bitch flying the helicopter was handling it like a constipated grandma. Mark and Luke were both complaining about getting airsick. Worst of all, the redneck detective and the bimbo racecar driver were still outpacing them.

He leaned out the window to fire another few rounds at the car below. The wind was strong enough to rip the bandage away from his wounded ear. He growled in frustration and fired again. At this speed, he couldn't even see where the bullets hit. The only thing he knew for sure was that they weren't doing jack shit to slow down that race car. The Uzi wasn't the right tool for the job and neither were the shotguns Mark and Luke had. If the weapons were going to be effective at all, they'd need to get closer.

Matthew eased himself back into the passenger seat and slammed the window shut. He turned his gun on the old fart pilot.

"I'm telling you right now, old man, if you don't stop flying this whirlybird like you got your thumb up your ass, I'll blow your head off!" He had to shout to be heard over the noise of the rotors. His throat was raw from the effort.

"What the hell, man?" Luke whined from the backseat. "You shoot him, who's gonna fly this thing?"

"Shut the fuck up!" Matthew reached into the pocket of his windbreaker and pulled out his grenade. "We're gonna get close enough to drop this bad boy right on their ass!"

Both the lunkheads in the backseat erupted at once.

"You got a hand grenade? What are you thinking?" Luke wailed.

"I don't want to be here no more!" Mark added, sounding like the world's biggest toddler.

Couple of goddamn sissies, Matthew fumed.

He elbowed the pilot in the ribs. "Take us down next to that car! And don't give me any bullshit or I swear on my mother that I'll blow your head off!"

The old man nodded furiously and took the chopper even lower. He goosed the throttle until they were even with the car.

Matthew couldn't believe what he was seeing. That racecar driver broad had her goddamn tits out and was shaking them like a stripper.

What the hell is wrong with these people? Matthew wondered. *Am I the only sane person left in the world?*

"Holy shit," Luke marveled. "Look at the fucking rack on that chick!"

Mark's airsickness wasn't enough to prevent him from leaning over Luke to get a better look. "Damn, man! You think those are all natural?"

Matthew hefted the grenade. It wasn't much bigger than a baseball, but it was a heavy son of a bitch. He thought about yanking the pin and dropping it onto the car like a bomb, but quickly reconsidered. Hitting a moving target at well over 100 miles per hour was a one in a million shot, and he only had one grenade. He had a better idea.

"Take us back up!" he shouted, gesturing to the pilot.

The old fart's shoulders sagged with relief as he pulled the chopper back to a reasonable altitude. He must have thought the chase was being called off. But he didn't know Matthew. Giving up wasn't an option he ever considered.

"Hey, old man." Matthew leaned closer to the pilot so he wouldn't have to shout quite as loud. "Take us that way, over that mountain. You see where the road curves just ahead of it?"

The pilot nodded.

"Set us down on the road where that curve straightens out," Matthew said, pointing at a spot in the distance.

His stomach lurched as the helicopter banked right. He braced himself for the sound of the idiots in the backseat puking, but miracle of miracles, those dumbasses managed to keep their breakfasts down.

The old man obeyed Matthew's orders, cutting across the open desert and landing the helicopter in the middle of the road just ahead of the long curve. Matthew brandished the gun at him and told him to stay put and keep the engine running.

"You do as you're fucking told and you might just live through this!" he shouted, then opened the door and jumped down to the cracked asphalt.

"Don't worry," the pilot said, giving him a thumbs-up. "I'll be here waiting."

Mark and Luke wriggled their massive bodies out of the backseat and nearly fell on their faces. They looked unsteady on their feet, but at least they weren't puking their guts up. Matthew motioned for them to follow him, and the three men ducked low as they ran clear of the helicopter. Once they were a safe distance from the whirring rotor blades, Matthew called them to a halt.

"Okay," he said. "Here's what we're going to do…"

Mark and Luke leaned forward, their brows furrowed as they prepared themselves to process simple instructions. But Matthew never got a chance to deliver those instructions, because he heard the sound of the helicopter beginning a quick ascent. He spun around and saw the chopper rise, its nose dipping slightly downward as it left the ground behind.

"What the fuck?" Matthew fired the Uzi in the helicopter's general direction, even though he knew it was pointless. In seconds flat, the old man had the whirlybird a hundred feet in the air, moving back across the desert.

Mark and Luke turned in circles, like they were trying to figure out what the hell was going on. Boiling with rage, Matthew fired at the rapidly receding helicopter.

"You old son of a bitch," Matthew raged. "I hope you have a heart attack and crash that goddamn thing!"

In all the commotion, he'd managed to pull out the stitches in his ear. Warm blood trickled down his neck. It only pissed him off all the more. He stomped back and forth across the road, screaming incoherently. Spit flew from his mouth. The veins in his forehead throbbed. His vision went red and his ears were filled with a high-pitched whine. And that's why he never heard Mark and Luke hollering for him to look out.

Cody took the curve without easing back on the gas. The Chevy handled like a dream. Mario and the rest of June's pit crew had done amazing work on the car. Everything about it was in tip-top condition. But even top of the line brakes can't halt a car doing 150 in time to avoid hitting man standing in the middle of the road only a quarter mile away.

"Shit, look out!" Cody cried, bracing himself for what lay ahead.

The Chevy hit Matthew dead-on, sending the fat man airborne. He flew twenty—hell, thirty—feet in the air before hitting the ground, splattering pieces of himself all over the asphalt. And then, inexplicably, what remained of him exploded, filling the air with red spray. It was like some explosive—a grenade or a stick of dynamite—had detonated beneath him.

Cody and June were spared the gory details as the Chevy fishtailed and went sailing off the road. There had only been one roadside sign for miles, and they managed to smash right through it. With his adrenaline-sharpened vision, Cody saw that it was a faded wooden billboard advertising Big Wang's All You Can Eat Chinese Buffet just before the Chevy reduced the sign to matchsticks.

The car rolled once then came to a rest on the sandy ground. Steam billowed from the hood and the engine choked, rattled, and finally died altogether. Had the Chevy been a regular model, he and June would probably have sustained major injuries, perhaps even died. But racecars were modified to take that sort of punishment while keeping passengers more or less intact. Once they'd shaken off the initial shock, Cody and June climbed out of the car.

"Out of road and shit out of luck," Cody said, looking over the hood of the car at June. "You okay?"

"Hell, that was nothing," she said. "You should have seen that one I had two years ago at Fort Lauderdale. Now *that* was a crash."

"And I'd love to hear all about it sometime, but right now we got a couple of big doofuses with shotguns coming our way."

The force of the explosion was enough to know Luke and Mark flat on their asses. Bloody chunks of their former boss rained down all around them.

"I told that crazy motherfucker," Luke said, plucking a glob of bloody tissue from his hair. "Them grenades ain't nothing to play with."

"What do we do now?" Mark asked, shaking his head like he'd just walked through a spider web.

Luke grabbed his shotgun off the ground and heaved himself to his feet. "I'll tell you what we do. We kill Cody Abilene and his girlfriend, then we go collect our money from Mr. Harper. A two way split is a hell of a lot better than a three-way, right?"

Mark looked unsure, but he nodded.

"Come on," Luke said. "Let's go."

Abilene and the broad were fleeing into the desert at a dead run. Luke groaned inwardly. More fucking running. He hated cardio workouts. But "no pain, no gain" was as close as he came to a philosophy of life, so he pushed himself to go faster. Mark huffed and puffed beside him, mumbling between ragged breaths about how he wanted to break Abilene in half. Seemed like he didn't care for cardio either.

Abilene paused every now and then just long enough to fire a couple shots with his big-ass Dirty Harry gun. How a pencil neck like that guy could even manage to lift such a big piece was a mystery Luke couldn't fathom. He didn't bother returning fire. It was hard enough to keep up the pace without stopping to take aim and shoot.

About a hundred yards ahead of them, Abilene and the

broad made an abrupt right turn and started heading for a small rocky hill that rose out of the sandy expanse like a zit on the earth's ass. Luke hated the desert. Shit was flat for miles and then there's a pile of rocks just sitting there like it was custom made for those two assholes to dive behind.

"Hold up!" Luke called and slackened his pace until Abilene and the woman were out of sight. He grabbed Mark's arm and pulled him to a halt.

Mark raised his shotgun and fired. All he did was raise clouds of dust from the side of the hill.

"Knock that shit off," Luke said. "You ain't gonna hit shit from this far."

"What are they doing?" Mark huffed. "Not like we don't know where they're hiding."

"Waiting to ambush us, that's what. Look here, I'm going to creep up on the right side of those rocks. When I got their attention, you run in from the other side and shoot them in the back."

"Sounds sorta like cheating…" Mark shrugged. "But what the fuck? I'm tired of running around out here."

Cody pulled June behind the jagged rock formation. They ducked low while the remaining Apostles popped off a few shots in their direction.

"We're in a tight spot," he said.

"No shit, cowboy." June rolled her eyes. "I suppose you got a plan for getting us out of this, you being a hotshot detective and all."

Cody broke open the .44's cylinder and spilled the spent shells onto the ground. He patted all his pockets and only came up with one bullet. He loaded it into the gun and told June the bad news.

"Well, babe, it's like this. I only got one bullet left and I've never hit a moving target in my life." He popped his head up just long enough to check their situation, then dropped back down. Luke was approaching at a steady clip, his shotgun held out before him. Cody dropped back down. "Shit, here he comes."

"Okay, if you don't have a plan, I do," June said. "Just follow my lead. I'm going to stop that target from moving."

She unzipped the top of her coveralls then sprang up just as Luke came around the side of the hill. Shaking her goodies like her life depended on it, which Cody supposed was entirely accurate, she called out, "Hey, big guy, look at these!"

Luke froze, hypnotized by the sight of June's D cups. He almost smiled before shaking his head to snap himself out of his trance. But that moment of tit-hypnosis was enough for Cody to make his move. He raised his gun, took aim, and fired. The shot punched a bloody hole through Luke's left side. The guy was a physical specimen, but even muscles like his weren't enough to stop a bullet. The shot dropped him like bag of moldy tangerines.

Cody sprinted over and grabbed the shotgun before Luke could recover. Once he got to Luke's side, he realized that recovery wasn't in the big guy's immediate future. The wound in his side might not have been mortal, but it sure as hell had him incapacitated.

"Look out behind you!" June called.

Cody spun around just in time to see Mark taking aim with his shotgun. Cody was faster on the trigger. He fired one shot, then another. The second caught Mark in the knee. For such a big guy, Mark screamed like a little girl as he collapsed onto the rocks. Squealing in pain, he clutched his shattered knee with both hands. June trotted over and grabbed his discarded shotgun. She finally had a chance to zip her breasts back into her jumpsuit.

Despite the circumstances, Cody was disappointed. He was always sad to see those beauties hidden behind a fabric barrier.

But he supposed that stuff would have to wait. He turned and looked down at Luke, whose eyelids fluttered and then slowly opened.

Cody aimed the .44 right at the big man's head. In his best Eastwood growl, he said, "Now, I know what you're thinking. Was it five shots or six? Well, you feel lucky?"

Luke squeezed his eyes shut again, his face contorting in a mask of pain.

Cody pulled the trigger. The hammer clicked as it fell on an empty chamber. He laughed as he watched a wet stain spread across the crotch of Luke's pants.

"Fuck you," Luke gasped.

Cody shook his head and clucked his tongue like a disapproving kindergarten teacher.

"Now, now. You be nice and we'll try to remember to send an ambulance this way for you and your buddy." He turned and waved at June. "Come on, sweetheart. Let's get out of here."

They headed for the old highway, leaving the two wounded bodybuilders behind. Cody emptied the shotguns, pumping the remaining shells into the dust. He tossed the guns in the opposite direction.

"Guess they won't need those anymore," he said, taking June's hand. "You know, your gorgeous front porch really saved our asses back there."

"I guess you owe me one, huh?" she laughed.

Chapter Thirteen

The Chevy was toast. Without some engine work, there was no way it was going anywhere. Cody retrieved Bev's purse from the car.

"Looks like we're still in business," he said, hanging the purse on his shoulder.

"You still haven't explained that purse," June said. "Is it a new fashion statement or something?"

"It's a long story, babe. Maybe I'll tell you someday."

Cody was just resigning himself to a long walk back to the raceway when spotted an RV approaching from the north. This RV wasn't some dinky little Airstream trailer; it was a top-of-the-line luxury vehicle.

"Hey, June," he said. "You feel like hitchhiking?"

"You mean in that thing?"

"Sure, why not?" He shrugged then stuck out his thumb. "Might as well ride in style. Gotta figure a way to get them to stop, though. Nobody much likes hitchhikers these days."

"I know how," June said, tugging at the zipper of her jumpsuit.

Cody couldn't do much but laugh. For the second time in the space of a few minutes, June was using her physical assets to bail them out of a tough spot. Waving her hands over her head and hollering like a cheerleader after the winning touchdown, June gave the driver quite a show. The RV's brakes were in good working order. It went from cruising speed to a dead stop before June's melons were done bouncing.

The passenger side door swung open, and Cody trotted up alongside the RV, eager to get

a look at the people who stopped to pick up a dirty, bedraggled private eye with a woman's purse and a half-naked female racecar driver. He'd expected a group of beer-brained idiots heading for a bachelor party or maybe some rock 'n roll band on the way to their next gig. He certainly didn't expect the husband-and-wife pair who smiled down at him from their fancy leather seats. They looked like they'd stepped out of a travel brochure for Nowhere, Kansas. The man wore a bowling shirt and a fishing hat. He looked like he knew his way around a buffet. His female partner—the guy's wife, Cody assumed—was resplendent in a shapeless floral-print blouse and sensible slacks. Her hair was swept up in a complicated arrangement atop her head. It was pulled back so tightly that her forehead was stretched and shiny.

"We must be getting close to Hollywood, Bill," the woman said, her eyes wide as she stared at June. "You don't see that sort of thing back home, that's for sure."

"You can say that again." The man leaned forward in his seat to get a better look at June.

Cody cleared his throat and elbowed her in the ribs to remind her to zip her tits back into her jumpsuit. She didn't take the hint and just stood there with her goodies on full display, grinning like she was holding back the punchline to a private joke.

"Hey, folks," he said. "I don't guess we could trouble you for a ride into town. We've had a bit of car trouble."

The woman turned to her husband. "Well, Bill, it wouldn't be right to leave them stranded out here."

He nodded enthusiastically. "You're right. It wouldn't be Christian. You folks climb in. We'll get you into town."

"God bless you, sir," June said.

The man smiled, staring at her breasts with mingled admiration and disbelief. "Well, ma'am, he certainly blessed you."

Cody glanced sideways and whispered, "Damn it, June, would you put those things away?"

They climbed aboard before the vacationing couple had time to develop second thoughts.

Bill and Betty Gardner from Olathe, Kansas were taking a cross-country vacation in their newly purchased RV. They'd seen four state parks, the world's largest ear of corn, the Grand Canyon, two museums devoted to antique automobiles, and one authentic Wild West show. They'd eaten at Howard Johnson's at least a dozen times and had worked their way through the entire Shoney's menu. Now that their kids, Geraldine and Kevin, were off at college, the Gardners had been living life like it was one long honeymoon.

Betty and Bill took turns narrating this story as they drove the RV back to Willow Springs. While Cody might have normally been bored to tears with such a tale, it was actually nice to have a bit of normality injected into the day's events. It was a sort of lucid interval between the car chases and shootouts. And June managed to refrain from disrobing during the entire ride.

Before dropping them at a 7-11, Bill gave Cody and June his business card and told them to give him a call if they were ever in Olathe and found themselves needed a quality used vehicle or a refurbished kitchen appliance.

"Got big lot just off Old Highway 56," Bill explained. "Big King Kong statue right out front, you can't miss it."

Cody tucked the card into his pocket and thanked them

again. "You folks have a safe trip. You make it to Disneyland, tell Donald Duck I said hello."

Once the Gardners had left to resume their tour of the American West, Cody sent June off in search of a sporting goods store that sold hollow point ammunition for a Colt .44, then he dropped a coin into a pay phone and called direct to Bev's office extension.

"Hey, pretty lady," he said when she answered on the second ring.

"Cody, thank God. Where are you?" she sounded tired but otherwise okay.

"Oh, hell, it's just a scratch. The doc gave me a couple stitches and some Tylenol. I had worse at Girl Scout Camp when I was a kid. So what's up?"

"Listen, I'm at the 7-11 in Willow Springs, just a few miles south of the raceway. June Khnockers is with me. In a few minutes, we're going to walk down to the raceway to get my daddy's car back. If you're feeling up to it, I need you to drive out there and pick June up. She's got your purse."

"Sure, I'm up to it. But what are you going to do?" Bev asked.

"I'm going to pay our pal Jonathan Harper a visit."

Bev groaned. "Oh, sure, you just charge off into battle and leave us little ladies behind? I don't think so, cowboy. This is the twentieth century, not the Wild West. Wait for me at the race track. I'll bring backup and we'll scoop up Harper together."

Cody considered the offer for moment, then decided it was to anticlimactic for his style. He wanted to see the look on that smug bastard Harper's face when he realized how much shit he was in. And Harper wasn't the only one Cody wanted to look in the eye, either.

"Sorry, Bev," he said. "But I'm going ahead with my plan. If you're too angry, you can take it out on me later."

He hung up before she had a chance to protest.

Jonathan Harper liked to think he knew how to throw a party. In his line of business, it was a vital skill. You wanted investors to open the checkbook, you had to show them a good time, let them know how much you appreciated them. It was a colossal pain in the ass, but sadly it was a pain that was entirely necessary. That was why he'd transformed the second floor conference room into a scene that would have made Hugh Hefner blush. The call girls outnumbered the guests three to one. The champagne, caviar, and cocaine were all top-shelf. The big screen TVs were showing hardcore porno and the stereo system was blaring the *Footloose* soundtrack. Among those circulating through the room were executives from film studios, oil companies, and Wall Street investment firms. In addition to the white collar criminals, there were a few shady operators from Eastern Europe and Central America. If only half of them decided to invest, Harper Technologies would soon be on its way to the Fortune 500.

He was seated on one of the room's leather couches, sipping Dom and admiring the action on the screen of the nearest TV. Nestled beside him was his favorite investor, Liza Chamberlain. Only she didn't seem to be enjoying herself very much. She had her arms crossed over her chest and was staring at him with undisguised disgust.

"Oh, don't tell me you're prudish about this stuff," he laughed, gesturing at the screen. "That particular movie stars your old butler Shane before he so tragically passed away. And I know she's your sister-in-law, but you gotta admit that Anita has a real dramatic flair."

"I don't like it one bit," she snapped. "And I don't like your despicable friends."

"Hey, these are upstanding and very wealthy citizens." He pointed across the room. "See that bearded gentleman with his face buried in that woman's crotch? His cousin is friends with the Saudi royal family. You hear what I'm saying? He's friends with a genuine fucking prince. So don't get all high and mighty."

Liza sniffed. "You're awful. You get me out here for an investors' gala and the first thing I see is Anita having sex with that jerk chauffeur. And I look around and see nothing but gangsters and Hollywood sleazeballs. You've got some nerve, Jonathan. I'm beginning to think my aunt was right about you."

"Come on, don't be that way."

Liza slapped the arm of the couch. "I want to know what you've gotten me involved in."

Jonathan dismissed her with a wave of his hand. If Liza wanted out of the business, that was fine. After tonight, he wouldn't need her anymore. Compared to most of the partygoers, she was small potatoes. He was so close to the finish line that he could taste it. Of course, that was usually when things got most fucked up. That saying about how it's always darkest before the dawn? Well, there was a flipside to that coin. And that's why Jonathan wasn't surprised when the door swung open and Cody Abilene strolled into the party with his gun drawn.

"Oh, you gotta be kidding me," Jonathan moaned.

Cody took aim at the stereo and fired, blowing the plastic and metal guts right out of Jonathan's newly purchased Sony sound system. Liza shrieked, clapping her hands over her ears.

"All right, assholes," Cody shouted. "This party's over. Everyone move out!"

The collection of hookers and coked-up bigwigs stampeded for the exit. They cleared the room in seconds flat, leaving the mingled stink of expensive cologne, spilled booze, and cigarette smoke in their wake. After hours of noise, the silence in the room pressed down on Jonathan like a wet rug. But he'd be damned if this hillbilly detective was going to intimidate him. He came off the couch feeling like he could spit fire. Some of that was down to the cocaine, sure, but he was plenty pissed off.

Weren't those three morons—Matthew, Mark, and Luke—supposed to deal with this problem? What the hell was wrong with them that they couldn't take out one stupid rube from Texas? One thing was for sure, those assholes were going to have some explaining to do.

"Just what the hell do you think you're doing?" Jonathan demanded, jabbing his finger in Abilene's direction. "This is my property and you think you can just walk in and embarrass me in front of my investors?"

Cody swung a fist into Jonathan's gut, knocking out his wind and his bravado with one solid punch. Then he turned to Liza and asked, "Why'd you do it, huh?"

"Do what?" she asked, incredulous.

"Why'd you kill Shane?"

"What the hell are you talking about?" she demanded. "I didn't kill anybody!"

Jonathan forced enough air back into his lungs to say, "Liza, you don't have to listen to this nonsense."

"Look here, asshole." Cody leveled his gun at Jonathan's head. "I don't like you very much. So why don't you do yourself a favor and shut your trap? Just sit there like a good old boy and I might not blow your head off."

Jonathan opened his mouth to protest but thought better of it. From this angle, the gun pointed at his head looked enormous. All the cocaine in Columbia couldn't motivate him to take a bullet from that thing.

Cody turned his attention back to Liza.

"At the party the other night," he said. "You went into Shane's room and you not only stabbed him, but you shot him too. And then you made it look like your brother Stewart did it. Your own brother and you framed him for murder."

"You're full of it," Liza said. "You don't have any evidence."

Cody reached into his back pocket and withdrew a folded 8x10 photo. He tossed it onto Liza's lap. "Take a look at this picture. Still think I don't have any evidence?"

Liza's mouth worked but no words came out. She looked like a landed fish gasping for air. The door swung open again and parade of cops trooped in. They were led by a man who looked like he'd stepped out of some old Bogart film. He was wearing a fedora, a trench coat, and a scowl that looked like it might be permanent. Beside him was a blonde in a smart pantsuit. She was pretty, but she also looked like a ballbuster. The rest of the bunch were uniformed cops. They dispersed throughout the room, collecting evidence and helping themselves to refreshments from the buffet table.

"Jonathan Harper, I'd like you to meet Lieutenant Arledge and Detective Sergeant Beverly McAfee." Cody holstered his gun and gave the blonde detective a gentle hug. "Hey, Bev, I'm glad to see you up and around."

"Well, you know how it is," she said. "You can't keep a good cop down."

"I hate to interrupt this heartwarming scene," the scowling lieutenant said, "but would you like to explain to me what the hell is going on here, Cody?"

"Sure thing." Cody snatched the photo off Liza's lap and presented it to him. "I think you'll find this very interesting."

While Arledge studied the photo, Cody grabbed Liza's arm and hauled her off the couch. He reached into the pocket of his windbreaker and pulled out a pair of sheer pantyhose. He tugged the pantyhose over Liza's head and spun her around to face Arledge.

"See any resemblance?" Cody asked.

"I'll be damned." Arledge stepped forward and held the photo up next to Liza's face. "Looks like a perfect match to me. Detective McAfee, you can do the honors."

"Liza Chamberlain and Jonathan Harper," Bev said, "you're under arrest. Please stand up."

Cody watched Bev slap the bracelets on Liza and Jonathan. He knew he should be happy. After all, there was nothing like saying "Case closed!" and going out for a couple celebratory beers. But there was something that didn't sit right with him. He couldn't quite put his finger on it, but something was tickling his investigator's brain.

"What's wrong?" Arledge asked. "I thought you'd be laughing it up and trying to distract Detective McAfee while she's doing her job. Instead, you look like your dinner doesn't agree with you."

Cody shook his head. "Tell you what, I need to go check on a few things. You guys look like you got everything under control here."

"You got nothing, Abilene. Nothing!" Jonathan screamed as Cody left the room.

Chapter Fourteen

Cody spent the next few hours at the Federal Technology Crimes office, giving Doug Wilton a full rundown of the week's events. But even as he narrated the entire tale, that same persistent brain itch kept tickling Cody. There was something he couldn't quite figure...

"Well, I'm sure it's nothing," Doug said, hitting the Stop button on the tape recorder. "It sounds to me like you wrapped up both cases at once. There's a good case against Liza Chamberlain for her role in that man's murder, and once we get done combing through Jonathan Harper's files, I'm sure we'll have a solid case against him for espionage. The CIA scooped up a few of his party guests, and they'll give up the goods once they start to get homesick."

"Yeah, it's just..." Cody sighed. "I can't shake this feeling like I'm missing something important."

Douglas pushed back from his desk and stood up. "As I said, I'm sure it's nothing. Go home and get some sleep. Everything will seem much better after you've rested."

"Yeah, maybe." Cody stood up and the two men shook hands.

"I'll be in touch," Doug said. "You did good work, Cody. Your country thanks you."

The sun was coming up when Cody finally left the office and slid behind the wheel of his daddy's Olds. As much as he'd have liked to agree with Doug's assessment that the case was closed, Cody just couldn't work his way around to it. Instead of going back to the marina, he stopped at Arlene's Malibu Diner for a cup of coffee and some pancakes with a side of bacon. But even with a jolt of caffeine and a couple thousand calories under his belt, his brain still hadn't managed to zero in on any loose ends.

"Anything else, honey?" his waitress, a cute redhead named Peggy, asked. She leaned over the table to clear away his dishes, making sure to angle herself just right so he could get a look at her cleavage.

"No, I think I've had enough coffee for one week. What's the damage?" he asked, reaching for his wallet.

"Well, honey, that breakfast is going to set you back one portrait of Abe Lincoln and whatever you feel like tipping."

And then, finally, the penny dropped.

"Portraits... pictures... *photos*," he said, shaking his head. He took a twenty from his wallet and handed it to Peggy. "Here you go, sugar. Keep the change."

Despite his exhaustion, Cody broke into a run as he crossed the parking lot.

In addition to the extensive engine work, Jimmy Dean Abilene's Olds was outfitted with every possible modern convenience, including a car phone. Cody used it to place two calls. The first one was to Doug Wilton.

"Cody, shouldn't you be home in bed?" Doug asked.

"Never mind that," Cody said. "I need you to do me a big favor, and please, don't ask me any questions. Go down to county lockup and get Liza Chamberlain out if she hasn't posted bail already. I just bet a guy like you, a guy who used to be a DA, can make that happen without ruffling too many feathers. Trust me on this one."

"You want me to spring the person you just had arrested for murder?" Doug's voice dripped disbelief. "Are you feeling okay?"

"You gotta trust me, Doug. Get her out and keep her under wraps for a couple hours, then bring her to my place. I have to check on a few more things, but I promise I'll explain everything."

"Okay, Cody, but..." Doug paused, sighing like a concerned parent. "I just hope you know what you're doing. If this thing doesn't go the way you want it to, I'm not sure I can keep going to bat for you."

"I read you loud and clear, but I'm one hundred percent on this one," Cody assured him.

His second phone call was to Contessa Luciana's house. As expected, there was no answer. That was okay. His business with the Contessa required a house call anyway. It took every ounce of restraint in his being to not stomp on the gas and speed across town to the Contessa's house. His mind was going a hundred miles per hour and the urge to match the car's speed to that of his thoughts was overpowering. But the last thing he needed was another speeding ticket, especially on a day like this, so he kept it to five over the limit and cursed every red light along the way.

Even though he was certain no one would answer, he rang the doorbell twice. Call it force of habit. Or maybe just call it his reluctance to resort to breaking and entering. Either way, he waited a respectful interval before whipping out his set of lock picks and getting to work on the front door. It didn't take him long to pop the lock. That was the thing about rich people: they tended to not have unbreakable locks. They relied more on private security patrols and fancy electronic alarm systems. Cody was lucky enough to not have to contend with the former at this hour of the morning, and the Contessa had been kind enough not to engage the latter.

"Guess I'm expected by the lady of the house," Cody muttered as he slipped into the foyer and kicked the door shut behind him.

The big house was as quiet as a tomb. It was that brand of silence particular to empty buildings, oppressive and almost spooky. Cody's footfalls on the hardwood floors echoed as he walked down the front hallway. He made a right turn into the sitting room where he'd waited while Luciana got ready for their night on the town. With the lights off, the room felt drab and cold. He groped along the edge of the wall until he found a light switch. He turned on the lights and glanced around the room.

It didn't take him long to find what he was looking for. Across the room, sitting on the carved wood countertop of the bar was a tape recorder and, hidden beneath a sheet of red fabric, an object about the size of a football. There was a card propped against the side of the tape recorder. The message on the card was simple: *Cody, play the tape. It will explain everything. All my love, Luciana.*

Cody pocketed the card and laughed. "Lady, you're way ahead of me. Probably been way ahead of me this whole time."

He hit the Play button. There was a brief hiss of static and then the Contessa's voice began speaking in her gentle, refined accent.

"Cody, by the time you listen to this recording, I'll be in Hawaii. I knew you wouldn't let an innocent person go to jail. After all, I did leave you some obvious clues, and I knew an analytical mind like yours would find them all. You may come on like a simple cowboy, Cody Abilene, but I know better…"

Cody smiled, shaking his head. *Luciana, you are one in a million.*

"I remembered the first time we made love," her voice continued. "Afterwards, you'd worked up quite a thirst. So after our next amorous encounter, after Lady Lillian's party, it was easy for me to give you a sleeping powder. I believe the phrase is 'slipping you a mickey.' Once you were fast asleep, I went to Shane's room and killed him. I disguised myself as Liza in case I was spotted or my image was captured by one of Shane's hidden cameras. When he snapped a photo of me before he expired, he only helped my plan along. I purposefully pried open his drawer from the right side, then intentionally took the wrong camera. I counted on you to figure out that the person in the photo was not Liza."

Contessa Luciana de Rossi, Cody thought, *you'd have been right at home with the Medicis and Machiavelli. Talk about intrigue...*

Luciana's taped explanation went on. "Shane was preparing to ruin the lives of people I loved. He was also a threat to the national security of the United States and a traitor to free people everywhere. I suppose you've also figured out that Shane was Jonathan Harper's courier for the Russians. I'm not just another pretty face. That's something we have in common, Cody. We're two of a kind, really. And that's why I know I can count on your discretion. I know you won't reveal that I work for an international government agency and that my contact in the United States is our mutual friend Douglas Wilton."

A regular female James Bond. Cody shook his head. *Will wonders never cease?*

The taped explanation rolled on. "I do feel a bit guilty for steering the police toward Stewart. It wasn't at all pleasant to have to send my friend Lady Lillian those awful photos of Shane and Stewart, but I knew that it would steer any suspicion away from me while I slipped out of town. Please convey my sincerest apologies to Lillian and Stewart. Now, please lift the red cloth off the object to the left of this tape recorder if you haven't already. You'll see how I was able to disguise myself as Liza."

Cody pulled back the cloth and revealed the most realistic mask he'd ever seen. It was so lifelike that just about anyone could have used it to masquerade as Liza Chamberlain. He touched it, marveling at the realistic texture of the material. It felt so much like real human skin that it gave Cody the creeps.

"As you know, I'm an artist," Luciana's voice said. "It's a shame that this is one piece that will not survive long enough to sit in anyone's collection, but I simply cannot allow any evidence of my involvement to remain. This is one piece of art that is for your eyes only."

As if on cue, the mask began melt into a pile of multicolored goo. Steam hissed as it rose from the slimy puddle. Cody leaned away, just in case that mystery material was toxic. The smell was certainly noxious.

"Two things have become very clear to me. The first is that I had you figured correctly. You're not only a very attractive man, you're also a very intelligent one. The second is that you'd help us get rid of Jonathan Harper. Thank you, Cody. Your country thanks you as well. And one more thing: I want you and your body here with me. I know you won't disappoint me on that score. I'm counting the days until you can join me. *Ciao, mi amore.*"

It didn't surprise Cody one bit when the tape recorder burst into flames, erasing Luciana's taped confession in a cloud of eye-stinging smoke. He stepped behind the bar and found a bottle of tonic water, which he used to douse the fire. Once he was sure the flames had been extinguished, he helped himself to a bottle of champagne from the small refrigerator beneath the bar. Closing a case this wild called for a celebration.

After he'd wrapped up his business at the Contessa's house, Cody used the car phone to place one more call, this one to his answering service. The voice that answered was breathy, sexy, and comforting in its familiarity.

"Sally's Phone and Lip Service, may I help you?"

"Hey, babe, it's your favorite client," Cody said. "I need you to get a few folks on the line and tell them to meet me at my boat in one hour. Think you can handle that?"

"Cody, I could handle anything you want to give me, no matter how big it is. You know I'm always ready to take direction from you."

"Girl, you're heaven sent," he said. "Okay, here's a list of the people I need…"

"Oh, yes, I hope it's a long list. I like it when they're long."

Despite everything, Cody had to smile. He gave her the list of names, thanked her again, and hung up the phone. He turned on the radio and found a station playing the new Van Halen single. No doubt about it, this day was shaping up to be a good one. Of course, whenever that seemed to be the case, something or someone showed up to throw a wrench in the machine. And that wrench was stamped with the words "P.L. Buffington and Family."

The hillbilly patriarch was driving an enormous Ford pickup. His son Bobo was riding shotgun, grinning like an idiot while using his right index finger to extract a particularly stubborn booger from his nose. Between these two prime examples of American manhood, sat Doreen, her face hidden beneath layers of drugstore makeup. The whole clan pulled up alongside Cody at a red light. P.L. laid on the horn to get Cody's attention, then began motioning furiously for him to roll down his window.

Cody took a deep breath and let it out with a sigh. He twisted the radio's volume knob, silencing Eddie Van Halen's guitar solo, then hit to button to lower the passenger side window. He leaned over the center console and shouted, "Hello there, Buffington family. Would it surprise you to find out that you've picked a really bad time?"

All three of them started jabbering at once, bouncing around so excitedly that Cody was sure the Ford's shocks would give out. Most folks wouldn't have been able to make heads or tails of the overlapping layers of babble, but Cody happened to be fluent enough in their hillbilly dialect that he could get the gist of what they were carrying on about. It seemed that Bobo had acquired a new car—a Camaro this time—and wanted to try for a third victory over Cody.

"Look, as much as I'd love to get my revenge," Cody said, "I got places to go and people to see."

"Aw, is that right?" P.L. leaned out the window and spit on the road. "Mayhap you're just too chicken. Now what would your daddy think if I was to give him a call and tell him that his boy has got a yellow streak running all the way from the crack of his ass to the back of his neck? Huh? Think old Jimmy Dean would be happy to hear how you're defending the family's honor out here in California? Now we got Bobo's Camaro stashed on the side of the old state highway just a few miles yonder. Unless you want the whole racing world to know that Jimmy Dean Abilene's boy is a coward, you'll follow us over there."

Cody knew damn well he didn't have time to go race Bobo for the third time in one week. But he also knew that he didn't want to deal with his father's wrath if P.L. actually made that phone call. He sighed again and told P.L. to lead the way.

The stretch of road that the Buffingtons had chosen was a straight shot of two lane blacktop. They'd spray painted a finish line two miles ahead. At least it was going to be a short race. He pulled the Olds alongside Bobo's brand new Camaro. It was a nice car, Cody had to admit. Modified for street racing, it had a 6-71 GMC blower atop the hood. Cody figured there was a supercharger beneath that hood. The engine was loud as hell when Bobo revved it. The big boy bounced around in his seat, hollering incoherently and banging on the steering wheel with his meaty fist.

Cody just shook his head. Bobo had no idea what was coming. Mike and his crew had been tinkering around on the Olds for months, intent on making it the fastest thing ever built on a standard chassis. Of course, that meant making dozens of illegal modifications, including everything from imported Formula One parts to bits and pieces cobbled together from military aircraft engines. The rear propulsion system was more suited to pushing a rocket to escape velocity than it was to moving a four-wheeled vehicle down three miles of cracked blacktop. The Olds was equipped with tires made of an experimental polymer to keep them from melting down completely once the rear system kicked in.

P.L. fired his pistol in the air and the race was on. Bobo was fast off the blocks, jumping out to a quick lead. But then Cody engaged the auxiliary engine. The hatchback lifted to accommodate the massive exhaust system, which belched a dragon's breath stream of fire as Cody dropped the hammer. Gravitational force pressed against his chest, pushing him back in his seat. The scenery became a blur in his peripheral vision, and for a few seconds, Cody's reality warped into a strange new dimension where pure speed was a tangible thing.

He crossed the finish line and took his foot off the gas, letting the engine slow before he applied the brake. He spun the steering wheel, pulling the Olds into a 180, so he could watch Bobo limp to the finish. P.L.'s white pickup followed close behind.

Although Cody was running late to his own meeting, he couldn't pass up a chance to gloat. After getting spanking by Bobo twice in a row, it felt good to restore things to their natural order.

P.L. barely had the truck in Park before he dismounted, waving his arms in the air and screaming accusations of cheating at Cody.

"You done strapped a rocket to that car!" P.L. shouted. "That is an illegal modification. Hell, it's downright immoral. You ought to be ashamed of yourself. Ashamed!"

By then, Bobo and Doreen had emerged from their respective vehicles. They joined in the chorus, demanding that Cody grant them a rematch in a normal car.

Cody leaned out of the window and made calming gestures until their yapping quieted to a dull roar.

"Now, if you'll excuse me," he said, "I'm running late for a meeting. Good thing I got a fast car to get me there on time. If I had to rely on that Camaro, I'd be up shit creek without a paddle. Ain't that right, Bobo?"

P.L. stammered incoherently. His beet-red face looked like it might burst into flames at any moment. He tore the straw hat from his head, threw it onto the road, and commenced stomping it to smithereens.

"I'll make sure to pass along your regards to my daddy," Cody said, tipping them a salute.

He flipped the rear engine's kill switch. The exhaust pipes vented one final hiss as the hatchback dropped. Cody put the car in gear and headed back towards town.

Chapter Fifteen

All but two of the guests were already assembled on the aft deck of the *Malibu Express* when Cody arrived. The other two were hiding out in the galley until the time was right for their big reveal. Cody greeted them when he stepped inside to gather his champagne glasses. Then he stepped out onto the aft deck and popped the cork on Luciana's champagne. Once they'd all toasted the successful close of the case, Cody leaned against the rail and smiled at the small crowd Sally had summoned.

Lady Lillian was dressed to the nines. Despite still being confined to a wheelchair, her regal bearing radiated from her core. To her left stood Lieutenant Arledge and Bev. Across from them, June Khnockers lounged in one of the deck chairs. Her white bikini top strained to keep her endowments in check while she sipped a second glass of champagne. Cody didn't feel quite so underdressed when he saw Anita in her jeans and t-shirt.

"Stewart sends his regrets," she said, raising her glass at Cody. "He had a lunch date with a, well... let's say a close friend."

"Okay, folks, we'll get down to business in just a moment,"

Cody said. "But first, we need to welcome two very special guests."

He crossed the deck and banged on the back door with his fist. A moment later, the door swung open and the final two guests stepped onto the deck. Liza came first, greeted by gasps of astonishment from the others. Doug followed close behind.

"You all know Liza," Cody said. "And right behind her, looking far too serious for such a joyful occasion, is Douglas F. Wilton, former D.A. and current high-ranking government official.

Oh yeah, he's also president of my daddy's yacht club."

"What's the meaning of this?" Lieutenant Arledge huffed. "We just arrested her last night."

Cody raised a hand before Bev could join in her boss' objections. "Okay, ladies and gentlemen, make yourselves comfortable while I do some explaining."

"Yeah, please do," June said, "because I gotta admit I got no idea what's going on."

"Here goes…" Cody smiled, drawing out the suspense for a couple more beats, then launched into his tale. "After the busts at Harper Technologies, I spent hours doing a debrief with Doug at his office. Something about the case kept bugging me, but I just couldn't figure out what it was. About an hour later, I had Doug go down to county lockup and spring Liza."

"But how did you know I was innocent?" Liza asked.

"I stopped for a cup of coffee and had an epiphany, I guess you could call it," Cody explained. "In all the excitement and with Harper's thugs chasing me, I didn't have a chance to really look at that photographic evidence I'd been carrying around. Once I finally got a chance to study it, Liza's innocence was clear as day."

"Now wait a second," Arledge interrupted. "I saw that photo myself, and the woman in it looked just like this young lady right here."

Cody nodded. "Sure, but there was one big problem. Liza is a lefty, and the person in that photo is holding the gun in her right hand. Not only that, but the person who jimmied the drawers open in Shane's room did it from the right side. What kind of lefty shoots and uses a knife right handed? It couldn't have been Liza. Still, I knew our killer was a woman. Every man who might be a suspect is at least six feet tall. Judging by the doorframe in the photo, the killer couldn't have been that tall, at least when she wasn't wearing high heels."

Arledge shook his head. "I can't believe I missed that."

"Don't sweat it, lieutenant," Bev said. "I missed it too."

"And I still got no idea what's going on," June chimed in. "But this is even better than TV."

"So I started narrowing down that suspect list," Cody continued. "It could have been that maid, Marian, because I don't think she's smart enough to pull off a disguise that convincing. Lady Lillian has been in a wheelchair ever since her skiing accident, so she was off the hook. Anita was—excuse me for saying this, sweetheart, but you were plastered. I doubt you could have held a gun steady long enough to fire it. That left only one possibility: Contessa Luciana de Rossi."

"Luciana?" Lady Lillian gasped. "But I thought she was on your side."

"Well, that's complicated. There's some things I'm not really at liberty to explain, but I can tell you that Luciana was investigating Jonathan Harper for another matter. All her actions were related to that investigation."

Cody left it at that. Luciana had asked him not to blow her cover, and he didn't intend to let her down. He didn't want to spoil any future encounters they might have.

Doug cleared his throat. "The Contessa has the full support of the government in this matter. She won't face prosecution for her role in Shane's death."

"Don't forget that Shane was no saint," Cody added. "We all know about his blackmail scam, but he was also the pipeline between Harper and the Russians. The connections Shane made in prison helped him connect Harper with certain rogue elements with ties to organized crime in Eastern Europe. The details on that are hazy, but it's stuff that's above my paygrade."

"Rest assured that these leads are being followed up," Doug assured everyone.

"Followed up aggressively."

"No one had been able to get close enough to Harper's operation to prove anything," Cody explained. "But then Shane's murder brought in the police. The feds had to hang back or risk blowing their cover."

"And they arrested my nephew Stewart by mistake," Lady Lillian said.

Arledge and Bev exchanged guilty looks.

"Don't feel too bad, guys," Cody told them. "Luciana sent those photos to Lady Lillian to muddy the waters of the investigation and get the cops looking in the wrong direction. She knew that Harper would get a false sense of security and do something stupid. He was too cocky to lay low until things cooled off. So with Stewart in county lockup, Harper figured he was in the clear. Since he figured Liza was on the hook for Shane's murder, he only had one loose end to tie up: me."

"Okay, now I'm starting to figure it out," June said. "That's why those creeps were trying to kill us in the desert."

Confused murmurs rippled through the assembly. Cody held up a hand to quiet them. "Long story. But she's right. Marian was feeding Harper info about my movements. He sent two thugs out to the beach house to take care of me and Bev. He needed to get that film back so he could protect Liza. Well, protect her investment anyway. At the very least, he needed to knock me off, so I couldn't go public with what I knew. When his first attempt didn't work, he sent three more after us again at the raceway."

"Where Detective Sergeant McAfee bravely took a bullet in the line of duty," Arledge put in.

Bev waved off the praise. "It was just a scratch."

"Harper's thugs went after me and June," Cody continued, "but we gave them the slip out in the desert. Harper must have figured there was no way his best guys could miss, because he went ahead with his plans. He threw a big party for his foreign investors, and the creeps really came out of the woodwork."

"We swept up several Soviet operatives." Doug actually smiled when he delivered this bit of news. "Plus a few organized crime figures with ties to Eastern Europe. Harper's lapse in judgment blew the whole case wide open. What it boils down to is Harper got greedy and overeager."

"What was I thinking?" Liza slapped her forehead. "I should never have gotten involved with someone like that."

"Hey, don't beat yourself up about it," Cody said, patting her shoulder. "Between blackmail, murder, and espionage, I get the feeling you won't be hearing from Jonathan Harper again."

"The whole situation is just awful." Lady Lillian shook her head. "Greed is such an ugly thing. Still, it's a shame that Shane had to die. He was quite the butler and chauffeur. And you know how hard it is to find good help these days." She grabbed Cody's hand. "Except for you, Cody Abilene. You are a wonderful detective. One of the last true cowboys. You'd never fail to help a woman in distress, would you?"

Cody glanced around the deck. Bev, June, and Liza all flashed smiles back at him.

"Help a woman in distress?" He raised his glass. "Yes, ma'am, I certainly would."

His closing line—which couldn't have been any better if he'd practiced it a thousand times—was upstaged by the arrival of his neighbors, Faye and May. The boat's back door swung open, and the two bikini-clad young women burst onto the deck.

"Hey, Cody!" May waggled her fingers at him. "You havin' a party or something?"

"Yeah," Faye said. "I guess our invitation got lost in the mail, huh?"

Cody shook his head. Looked like it was time to upgrade his security system.

The following pages feature images from the film *Malibu Express*. Used by permission.

MALIBU
EXPRESS
CIC
VIDEO
SYBIL DANNING
EDIT
FRANCE
LES PLUS BELLES FILLES DU MONDE

MALIBU EXPRESS
Die schönsten Frauen der Welt
in einem heißen Abenteuer
DARBY HINTON
SYBIL DANNING
cic
VIDEO

NE KHNOCKERS

MALIBU
EXPRESS

MALIBU
EXPRESS

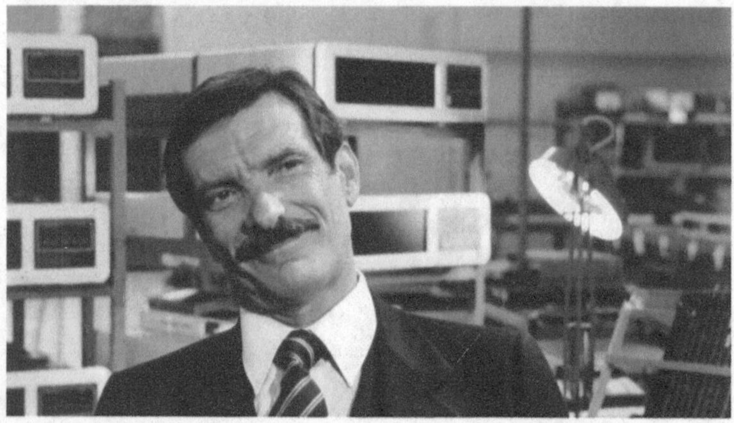

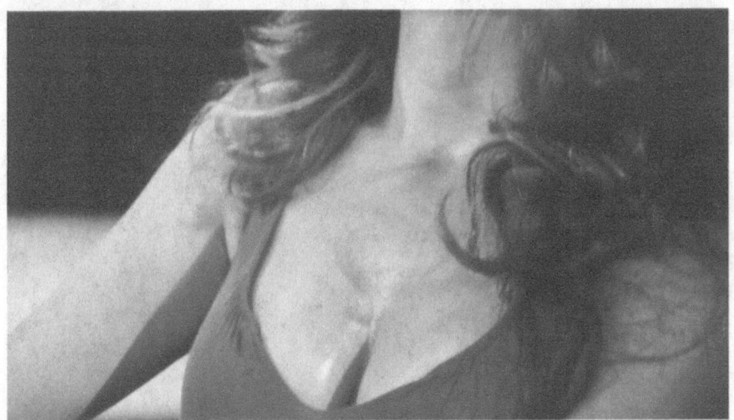

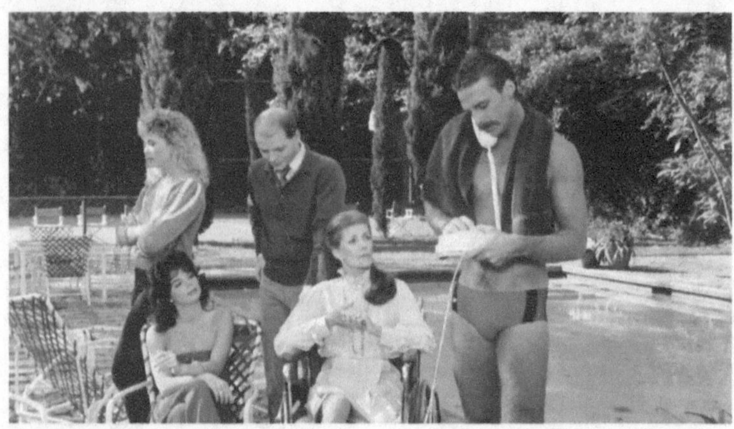

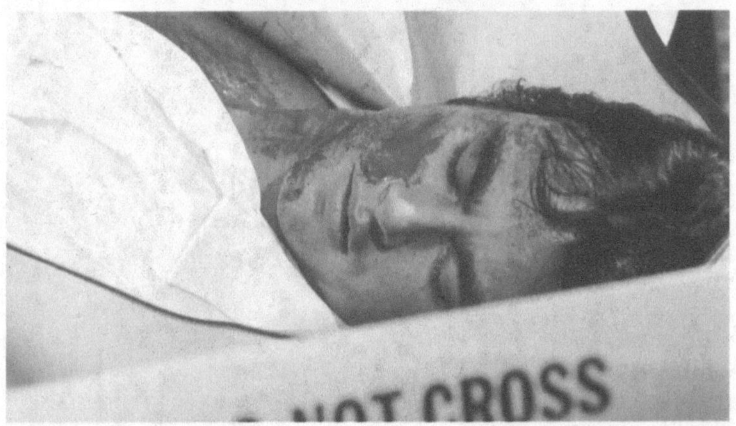
NOT CROSS

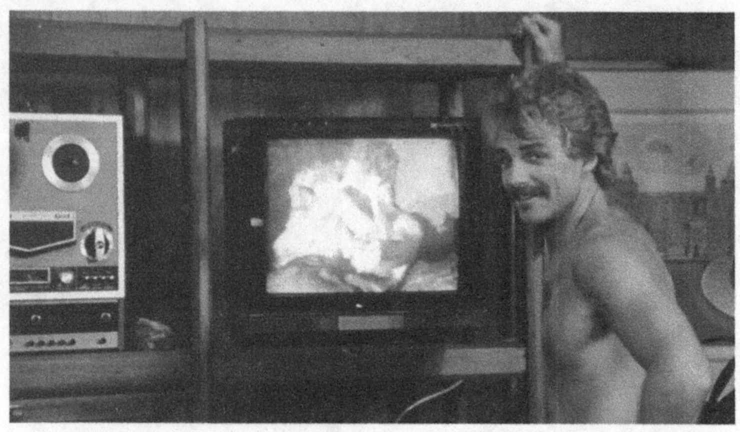

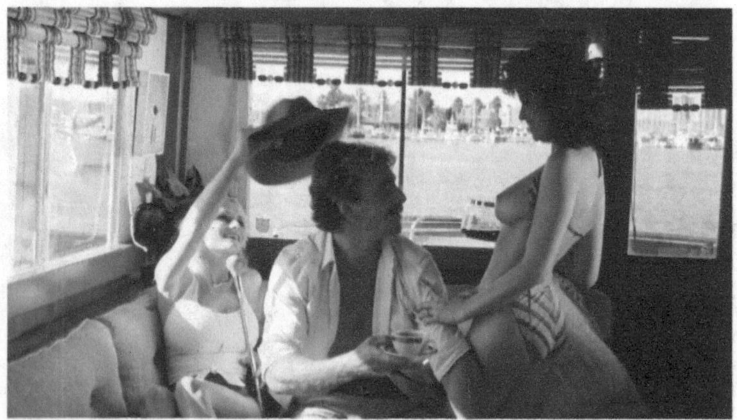

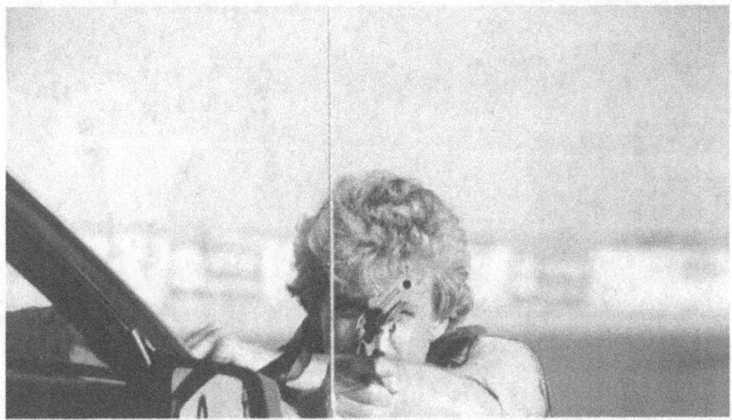

MALIBU EXPRESS

About the Author

Brad Carter lives in Arkansas with his wife and daughters. They encourage him to write, because it keeps him out of trouble.

Also from Brad Carter
(dis)Comfort Food
Saturday Night of the Living Dead
Only Things
Uncle Leroy's Coffin
Human Resources
Cruel Jaws
Rats: Night of Terror
Virus: Hell of the Living Dead
Hard Ticket to Hawaii